Fifties Chix: Till the End of Time

Angela Sage Larsen

Published by Premiere

Published by Premiere
307 Orchard City Drive
Suite 210
Campbell CA 95008 USA
info@fastpencil.com
(408) 540-7571
(408) 540-7572 (Fax)
http://premiere.fastpencil.com

This is a work of fiction. The author makes many historical references, but encourages the reader to do her own research to learn about the twists and turns history has furnished to bring us to this: the future.

Manufactured in the United States by Courier Corporation
46468601 2013

For my mom, who taught me what love is, how to expand my horizons and how they mean the same thing. When we meet again, we will have lots of catching up to do.
Love always.
And for my mother-in-law, Jo, for teaching me that "home is the center
. . . of the affections."
Love always.

❧

Acknowledgments

This is like a graduation; it feels a bit like an end, but it's just the beginning. But it's been a long and intense "commencement" and I'm grateful to be throwing my cap in the air with my editors Lori Van Houten and Liz Wallingford: you are graduating with highest honors! Thanks to the Premiere publishing team for playing "Pomp and Circumstance" over and over again —Bruce B, Marie, Mariena, Matt, Steve, Mash, and the whole band—what beautiful harmony you make! To the valedictorians of my life: Phebe, Kim, Trish, Leah, Kendra, Candy, Michele, both Karens, and Jennai; you are infinitely talented, brilliant women who inspire me every day. I'd like to acknowledge my family, too, for being such an active cheering section: Bumpa/Grandpa, Dad, Cynthia, Bruce, Valerie, Ryan, Bob and Jo, and all my in-laws, nieces, nephews, and cousins. And last, but never least, no one will ever know how selfless, supportive, and generous my husband Whit has been throughout this process—but I know. I am humbled and infinitely blessed to call him my best friend. Truly, "happiness cannot exist alone, but requires all mankind to share it" (Mary Baker Eddy).

Contents

1

It's Time

May Boggs rubbed her temples. She never should have told Reggie she wouldn't go to dinner with him. She had the weekend to grade papers. Her mother had warned her about becoming a career girl; she had told her to always put a man first. May turned the TV off. She couldn't concentrate with I Love Lucy on. If she had declined Reggie's invitation to work, then, by golly, she needed to honestly work.

But even with the television off, it was hard to concentrate on the stack of "Travel to Tomorrow" reports in front of her. Not only were the students' efforts dismal, she couldn't keep her mind off of charming Reginald Fairview. Besides the fact that he was everything her mother wanted for her—handsome, educated and from a good, wealthy family—he was everything May herself dared not ask for. He was kind, thoughtful, and supportive of her teaching career. He had already told her that if they ever were to marry, he'd never ask her to stop teaching if that was what she wanted to do.

May gazed dreamily out into the evening through the lacy curtains she'd put up in her apartment a few months earlier. Maybe this weekend he would ask her. She would say yes, of course. Mrs. Marion Gertrude Fairview. She mentally savored what her new name would be. She mused about dropping the Gertrude . . . how about Mrs. Marion B. Fairview? She loved it. Her heart leapt.

But with her line of work, she needed to be careful. No personal attachments. That's why her apartment was so empty of treasures, knickknacks, or anything sentimental. She walked a fine line with Reggie. The fact that he didn't mind her teaching career, well, maybe it meant he could deal with her other calling. . . .

With a sigh and a great deal of resolve, May adjusted her cat-eye glasses and turned her attention to her students' projects. She had high hopes for Mary Donovan, Judy White, Maxine Marshall, Beverly Jenkins, and Anna Branislav. They each had such interesting backgrounds and unique perspectives; in fact, they had actually inspired her idea for the "Travel to Tomorrow" project.

She hoped their reports were better than their presentations had been earlier that day. When they'd been in front of the class, May had wondered if they had understood at all the point of the project. But seeing them after school at the five-and-dime had warmed her heart. She had made them promise to be friends in another half a century. Marion knew how fleeting youth and idealism could be; if she could do anything as an educator, she wanted to give her students hope for the future, as she and her two best friends had been given hope from the past once upon a time.

Well, she was about to find out if she had given hope to those five girls . . . .

After reading and re-reading the girls' papers, May carefully removed her cat-eye glasses, which had gotten a little steamy. She rubbed her temples. She surmised she would have to meet them after class the next day, but she knew deep down this wouldn't be enough. She reminded herself of why she had become a teacher in the first place.

No, a little teacher speech wouldn't be enough to inspire these five girls. She would have to take more extreme measures. She had mixed feelings about it . . . but she knew, in the end, their own personal "travels to tomorrow" would be for the best. It might be tough going at first, but wasn't that why she had made them promise to be friends at the soda shop earlier? It would all work out in the end.

May looked down at the ornate gold watch around her wrist, which she had been given for this very purpose—not that that fact made what she had to do any easier.

It was time.

Miss Boggs wound her watch and braced herself.

May 28, 2010

Emily Jackson's ballet "school"—a large room with a wall of mirrors in the lower ninth ward of New Orleans—was becoming more successful than she'd anticipated. Already she needed to think about a new location with more space and more amenities (like heat and air conditioning). But those things meant leaving this neighborhood. And Emily didn't want to lose these students by making them travel too far, raising the cost, or replacing her black students with white ones. She hadn't figured out a successful way to integrate her classes, even with all of her impassioned speeches about how ballet knows no color. Immediately following hurricane Katrina, there had been an onslaught of support; but after a year it had waned and she was back to fighting it out on her own. Well, on her own with her older sister, Viola.

The frustration lately was exacerbated by what she was now calling "waking dreams"—strange visions of faraway times, places and people crowding in as if two or more dimensions were colliding. Emily felt another spell coming on. *Not now*, she screamed silently. She could not have one in the middle of a ballet class that she was teaching, especially not this one—the ten-year-olds in ballet level four.

"*Retiré devant!*" Emily tapped her cane. She'd needed it since the first episode nearly a month ago, which had caused her to lose her balance and hurt her leg. The cane was good for support, but she used it to bang out rhythms for her students, too. She liked to pretend it was a shepherd's crook or a queen's scepter. She used it as both in class. "Now, *battement développé!*"

Emily gazed across a meadow of preteen ballerinas, their willow-like legs lifting and extending obediently, as if they were all being blown by the same gentle breeze. She focused on them to keep the vision at bay. They were real, now, here.

The spells were coming more frequently, but she refused to cancel class and she just as equally refused to fall into a waking dream. It would be too traumatic for her students to see what might happen to her if she conceded. And Vi was out of town for the weekend, so she couldn't depend on her for help. Em had insisted that Vi take a trip to St. Louis to see her son, Conrad, play in his big baseball games. Em knew that Vi also hoped to discuss a reconciliation with her estranged husband.

As hard as Emily tried, the image still crowded in: she was in another place, on a dangerously seething river, in a boat of desperate women in the middle of the night. How could it not be her own actual memory when she was able to smell the cold, muddy dankness of the rushing river, feel the bitter air stinging her cheeks and making her eyes water? She felt her feet blistered and pained but not from dancing, her hands raw from rowing. And her heart hurt, not just from being out of breath and exerting herself, but from something she had seen and experienced.

"*Relevé*," she called out to the class and demanded of herself.

At the end of class, her loyal and talented niece, Ginny, gave her Auntie Em a hug as she always did before waiting for her mama—Em's sister Viola—to retrieve her. But today she'd be staying at the studio until Em took her home for dinner to feed her and Ginny's brother and sisters. Em gave her an extra long squeeze.

"Did you have another waking dream, Auntie?" Ginny whispered, concerned.

Em wondered how she must have come across to her class and to her sweet little niece.

Ginny added, "Should we call Mama to come home?"

"No, gingersnap. She'll be back in two more days and I'll be fine till then. I have y'all to take care of me." Em kissed the top of Ginny's head, where a messy bun rested precariously among her black fly-away hair.

Em's next class didn't start for another thirty minutes. She took a deep breath to pull herself together, but like a flash flood knocking her off her feet, another image came. She sat at her desk and asked Ginny to get her some water. Head in her hands, she let the vision come into focus: a soda shop with two white girls, her heart full and laughter filling the space between them like a sweet fragrance. They were her best friends; Em knew that because of how she felt with them. They made her feel safe and bold at once. They were talking about a school project; Em suddenly filled with despair. Her friends offered help and advice. And then, as sometimes happens in sleeping dreams, the scene shifted suddenly. The same two girls were with her in someone's bedroom—the blond girl's. The other girl was showing them a remarkable gold watch . . . .

Em came to herself.

"Are you sure we shouldn't call Mama?" Ginny, standing over Em with a cup of water, asked worriedly.

"I'm just fine," Em consoled her. "It's getting better even though I know it must look scary. But I'm doing great."

Ginny held out the water and kept her distance. Em was sorry she'd frightened her. She hoped Ginny wouldn't call Viola behind Em's back. She had been telling Vi the same lie—that she was getting better—so Vi would take her trip to St. Louis.

Em was also tempering her reports of the visions to Vi because Vi's taste for the melodramatic tended to blow things out of proportion. Already overly fascinated with supernatural and paranormal phenomena, Vi almost relished Em's episodes, quizzing her on details—what Em had been thinking right before a flash occurred, what she'd eaten the day before, and other nonsenses that Em knew instinctively were not the causes. Vi was convinced that Em was a medium for some poor dead girl with unfinished business.

But Em knew the truth. She knew that she herself was the girl. She wasn't seeing someone else's life flash before her eyes; she was seeing her own. Which didn't make sense, because she was 26 years old, yet having "memories" of the 1940s and the Civil

War; it was like she was trapped between dimensions. Em had recently found a letter in an old trunk in her closet. She had wanted to run and show Vi, but she'd restrained herself. She couldn't take seeing Vi's big eyes widen as Vi hyperventilated over the spectacle of it all and pontificated her half-baked theories of spiritualism, necromancy, and divination. So until Em could prove what she suspected was true—that she was the intended recipient of a letter written in 1955—she kept it to herself.

She'd taken to carrying the letter with her in her bag and reading it frequently, as if by embracing it, she would spontaneously glean some kernel of truth from it.

By the time she'd recovered her breath, Em had only seven minutes until her next class and most of the advanced students were present and warming up. Em couldn't help herself; she retrieved the letter from her bag and ducked into the tiny water closet that was a poor excuse for a bathroom.

Taking several deep breaths, she unfolded the single delicate, yellowed sheet. It had clearly been thick, expensive paper, but was now brittle with age. Her heart thudded to the bottom of her stomach as it always did when she read it. The letter was short and typed:

```
July 11, 1955
Dear Emily,
   I received your letter dated June, 1955 in
due order. My apologies for not responding
sooner, but certainly you of all people under-
stand delayed responses. Since your letter,I
have gotten married to a wonderful man and
have started a new life. I hope you understand
```

what this means; I have put the past where it
belongs - behind me - and I am looking toward
the future. You should do the same, dear Emily.
There is not a place for you if you look to
the past, or to me or to Rowena.

 Too much time has passed to pick up where
we left off. Rest assured, all is well and I
wish you the best for a happy life.

 Sincerely,

 Mrs. Marion "May" Fairview

Em's hand covered her mouth to smother the sob that
escaped. But she reminded herself that she could bear the emo-
tional and even physical toll this all took on her because of the
simple hope that she held out: that someday she would know
who Rowena and Marion were and if they were girls in her
visions, and what it all meant.

2

Square One

Mary Donovan wasn't one for sleeping in, especially when her life was starting to make sense, like a puzzle that was coming together at long last. There were still missing pieces, but at least it was starting to take shape—corners and edges first, like Nana had taught her.

Having some sense of decency, she refrained from calling any of her friends so early in the morning. Instead, she spent the extra energy that had awakened her before dawn to set up her sewing machine and work on a project. She wanted to surprise her current events teacher, Mrs. Fairview, for her "It's Your Life" retirement assembly presentation. Mary had designed a quilt with 55 squares, one for each year that had passed since Mary, Ann, Bev, Maxine, and Judy had known Mrs. F. Of course, the then-Miss Boggs had started teaching three years before Mary and her friends had met her, but Mary reckoned Mrs. F would understand perfectly the 55 squares reference.

Since time was of the essence, Mary couldn't put as much detail into each square as she would have liked; some squares were just seamless fabric shapes, but some had more meaning with initials and forms stitched from fabric that Mary had from the 1950s. She crafted squares with appliqués of a baseball bat, a movie reel, a paintbrush, a feather quill, and the outline of her own sewing machine. She even made the center appliqué a gold watch, the face of which contained a big red heart. Mary knew it was all a bit self-promoting of the Fifties Chix, but she knew she'd have some fun details to add once they met with Mrs. F's husband, Reggie Fairview, later that day after church. And she'd have James O'Grady convince his Aunt Row, Mrs. F's best friend, to sign her name and Mary would embroider over it.

Since they had found out that Mrs. F's other best friend, Emily Jackson, had been a dancer, Mary thought she'd even stitch a ballet slipper from a swatch of petal pink satin she'd been saving for something special.

As for the rest of the "It's Your Life" presentation, Mary was still a little stumped about how it would come together, but she was counting on Judy's dramatic flair, Ann's artistic touch, and Maxine's talent for narrative to help her round it all out. Bev was a team player and would be amenable to whatever the others decided, Mary was sure. They had rallied countless other times, like with the newspaper for Maxine, *The Visible Truth*—and that one they had managed to produce with only a few hours' notice.

Mary got so involved with her project, she nearly forgot the time. She didn't want to miss Mass; today she had planned on getting up the nerve to sit with James. Mary powdered her nose, cleaned her glasses, and straightened her pony tail, then went to find Nana for a ride to church.

"You're in good spirits." Nana smiled knowingly as the two of them drove the short distance toward the remodeled chapel that Mary now called her church. Mary knew Nana thought that Mary was chipper because of James, but he was only part of it. She'd let Nana think what she wanted; it was too complicated to get into.

But Mary's spirits flagged upon entering the large auditorium and seeing that James was not in his usual spot. With her thoughts now focused on James, she didn't hear any of Father Steve's sermon. She reflected on how preoccupied James had been the last few days; he'd even missed her information-seeking visit to Mr. Twigler's the day before. He wouldn't have missed it unless something important or dire had come up; James had discovered, after all, that the school custodian—known as "Twig"—was involved with time travel research for the government. James wouldn't have missed an opportunity to grill Twig about that for the world.

And Mary hadn't gotten a clear answer from James, even after calling him four times and seeing him the night before. Now he was missing church. Mary was worried. She hoped he could still accompany her and the other girls to Mr. Fairview's house across town. The sermon dragged on; with each passing second, Mary fretted more.

By the time they said their final prayers and exited the over-sized wooden doors into the blazing sunshine, Mary was in a foul mood. She pulled her cell phone out of her purse, grateful that she was getting in the habit of bringing her phone with her. She pressed the button for James's number and got his voice-mail. Again.

She'd never been to James's house before and it felt too forward to drop by; but she didn't have a problem with dropping
by Aunt Row's house. If she ran into James there, perfect; if she
only got to speak with Aunt Row, that wouldn't be terrible,
either.

When Mary asked Nana for a lift to Aunt Row's, Nana rattled
off all the activities she was already shuttling Mary's younger siblings off to: Maggie and Patty had a dance recital and Danny had
T-ball practice. Mary's mom was getting a manicure and then
showing some houses. "But it's Sunday," wailed Mary. She
couldn't believe her little kid sisters and brother had a more
active social life than she did. On a Sunday no less. And whatever had happened to Sunday dinners as a family? Not that
she'd reserved the day for her family, but that wasn't the point.

"It doesn't all revolve around you, pumpkin," laughed Nana,
gently poking fun at Mary. But Nana had hit a nerve and Mary
didn't laugh with her. "I can drop you off, but I won't be able to
come get you for another three hours," Nana said.

Mary brightened. That wouldn't be so bad; she'd find James
by then and go to see Mr. Fairview and be back. Now she felt
like a goof for being such a sourpuss, so she remained polite,
thanking Nana and giving her directions to Aunt Row's.

Mary brightened when she saw James's car in the driveway.
She bolted out of the car, nearly forgetting her manners. "Oh,
sorry, Nana. Thanks for the lift!" She waved happily and tried to
keep herself from running through the gate and up the path to
Aunt Row's porch.

Knocking on the heavy wooden door, Mary contemplated
taking her hat and gloves off. It was Sunday, but no one else
wore a hat and gloves anymore on Sunday or any day of the

week. Plus, it was uncomfortably warm, even without accessories to further insulate her.

The door opened partway and Mary grinned when she saw James on the other side of it.

"Hiya!" she said.

"Hey, Mary," he said. There was a coolness to his tone, but it didn't take Mary long to realize that it had nothing to do with her.

"What's wrong? Is everything OK?"

He shook his head no and Mary saw that his eyes were bloodshot. He struggled to speak. "It's my Aunt Row. She's not well. It happened so suddenly . . . . We were having a family meeting and she just . . ." Mary waited and James choked out, ". . . collapsed."

"Oh, no," breathed Mary, her eyes filling with tears. James loved his Aunt Row. And so did Mrs. F. Mary wondered if she knew yet. Mary wanted to hug James, but didn't want to be too forward; but he opened the door and took a step onto the porch and embraced her.

He mumbled into her neck, but Mary missed most of what he was saying. "My fault . . . with parents . . . judge said, but I didn't just wait . . . so upset and argued with Row in the middle . . . ."

"I'm sure it's not your fault," Mary reassured him. "How can I help?"

". . . just feel so alone," James finished, straightening himself and wiping his eyes.

"You're not alone," Mary said. "You have me. And you have the rest of the Fifties Chix."

Through his tears, James managed a short one-syllable laugh. "The Fifties Chix?"

Mary blushed. "Oh, yes. We call ourselves that. It's silly, but . . . ."

"No, it's clever. I like it. It's fitting." James seemed to have needed to smile. Mary didn't want to ruin the moment by bringing in the fact that it was Diane Dunkelman who'd actually come up with the name. "Thank you, Mary."

"I haven't done anything yet."

"You have. Thanks coming by at just the right time and for reminding me that I'm not alone. I need to stick around here, but I'll keep you posted."

"OK. Say, does Mrs.—"

"Yeah, she knows. She's here." James tilted his head toward the interior of the house.

Reluctantly, Mary said her goodbyes and walked home in the heat. It wasn't the long walk or the burning sun that made her steps so heavy; it was the hollow ache she felt for James and for Mrs. F. And, of course, for Aunt Row. Mary felt helpless. The quilt she had been so jazzed to make for Mrs. F now seemed pointless and frivolous. What would Mrs. F do with a silly old quilt anyway?

Mary felt a bead of sweat form at the base of her neck and slither slowly down her spine. *What was it all for?* she began to wonder. If they had "traveled" to catch a glimpse, what were they glimpsing and what were they supposed to do with it? With each step, Mary found her pity slowly shifting from James and Aunt Row to her own plight. Her frustration at not being able to be much use at the moment had been a seed that quickly sprouted and grew into a prickly shrub of indignation.

By the time she got home, Mary's reason for visiting Mr. Fairview had changed from getting information about Mrs. F's life for her retirement celebration—while surreptitiously gleaning some insight into her connection to their time traveling—to demanding to know if he was aware that his wife was messing with everybody's lives.

"Back so soon?" Nana called as she hustled two costume-laden girls and a T-ball-uniformed boy out the door.

"Yeah, I saw James, but his—" Mary started, but saw that Nana wasn't listening.

"That's great, honey. We'll be back later. Have fun with your homework!" The door closed and in an instant, the house was quiet except for the whirring of the dishwasher, clothes tumbling in the dryer, and the kitchen clock ticking loudly.

. . . . *And another thing,* Mary's mental tirade continued, *if this was all temporary, when would it be yanked away from them?* She took her hat and gloves off and poured herself a glass of milk. Though the milk wasn't delivered fresh with a thick layer of cream anymore, she was starting to acquire a taste for the thin watery milk Nana now bought for the family. She sat at the kitchen table and pulled her little phone out of her purse. She called Judy first.

Before Mary could tell Judy the news about Aunt Row or ask her if they could get a ride to see Mr. Fairview, Judy was gushing.

"Guess what?" Not waiting for Mary to guess, Judy continued excitedly, "It turns out Roger Streeter—that's my mom's steady —was a theater major in college! Mom is finally introducing us today and he's going to help me prepare a piece for my audition tomorrow!"

"That's terrific—"

"Oh, I know; we were going to see Mr. F today. You and the girls will have to go and tell me all about it. Thanks for understanding, Mary; you're the most. Maybe Roger won't be so bad, you know, like your stepmom-to-be. What's her name?"

"Tiffani."

"Righto, like Tiffani! I'll keep you in orbit!" Judy clicked off and Mary realized she had barely gotten three words in.

With a sigh, she dialed Maxine's number. Mary knew Maxine was eager to get to the bottom of their time travel quandary.

"Hi Maxine, it's Mary."

"Oops, hold on. It's Mel here." Maxine's sister told Maxine to keep it brief as she passed the phone to her.

"Heya, Mary."

"Hi. Are you going somewhere?"

"Yeah, actually; Mel invited me to this poetry slam at a coffeehouse. I don't know much about it, but it's all very beat. She liked some of my poems and thought I should read some."

"That's great. Will there still be time to go to Mr. Fairview's with us?"

"You know what? I totally forgot!" Maxine said and Mary relaxed. She knew Maxine would change her plans back to go talk to Mrs. F's husband; but instead, she said, "I'm so sorry, Mary, I'll have to sit this one out. Let me know how it goes. Then maybe we can try to talk to Aunt Row."

"Aunt Row . . . actually, she's not well." Mary explained her conversation with James and hoped that Aunt Row's condition might change Maxine's mind about going with her sister to the coffeehouse.

"What can we do for Aunt Row?" Maxine asked, concerned.

Mary racked her brain to think of something, but came up with nothing. "I guess we just wait and see."

Maxine made sure Mary would keep her updated and they got off the phone.

Mary's next call was to Ann. As the phone rang, she felt guilty. Was calling on a Sunday—

"Hello?"

"Mrs. B, this is Mary."

"Hello, sweetheart." Mary liked being called sweetheart by Mrs. B; it stirred her memory of the time they had met in 1955 when Mrs. B had made cupcakes for one of the Fifties Chix' first meetings at Bev's house.

Mary asked after Ann and was surprised to learn that Ann was with Gary Jenkins. Gary was writing a paper and needed Ann's help, Mrs. B explained. Mrs. B assured Mary that she'd give Ann the message that she'd called.

Mary didn't begrudge any of her friends their fun, but she was disappointed that it was down to just Bev and her to go talk to Mr. Fairview. She'd been convinced that there would be power in numbers; and it hadn't occurred to her that her friends' priorities could change so quickly.

Mary dialed Bev's number, and there was no answer except for a recorded message. Though Mary had left recorded messages before, she didn't like to do it and she hung up quickly before having to speak.

Stunned, she listened to the whirring appliances and the mocking tick-tock of the clock. Panic began to rise in her, choking her and blurring her vision. This was worse even than fighting with her friends. She felt all alone and like she was back at square one.

3

Catch-22

Beverly Jenkins doubled over with laughter. She had no idea Conrad was so funny. She had been wolfing down a PB and J for lunch when he'd shown up on her doorstep and asked if she wanted to have a catch. Hoping that she didn't have peanut butter crusted in the corners of her lips, she'd smiled a happy, "Sure!"

Bev had hesitated only for a moment after that, wondering who she should tell that she was going out, but no one else was home. In the past, Pops had always been around on Sundays because his store was closed, but now he worked crazy hours almost every day of the week for a store he didn't even own. Bev jotted a quick note and stuck it to the fridge:

Out to play catch with Conrad.
- Bev

Bev grabbed a baseball cap, a mitt, her bat, and a ball. Conrad laughed at all that she carted with her, saying, "I did bring a ball," but she brought her stuff with her anyway. On the way to the park, they'd compared notes about their games the day before —Bev having played with the girls' softball team and Conrad having gone to State playoffs with the boys' baseball team. They'd already talked about it at the diner the night before, where she and her friends had gathered to celebrate and Conrad (and Bob and Gary Jenkins) had joined them. As had Diane Dunkelman.

Now, as they stood in the wide, grassy expanse of a nearby park, the sod still green before the oppressive summer heat deadened it to distressed brown, Bev and Conrad tossed the ball back and forth and with each throw, they called out the worst smell they could think of. Bev didn't know how they'd started it, other than that she'd said she felt like she lived in a boys' locker room every day of her life because she had four brothers. She and Conrad tried to outdo each other so that the other would miss or drop the ball. Conrad was winning, but Bev hadn't dropped the ball yet; he was just funnier.

After an hour, when they had worked up a sweat, Conrad asked if she was up for ice cream.

"Always," Bev replied.

They drove a short way to a frozen yogurt shop and Bev gasped. "This used to be—" She stopped herself.

"Used to be what?"

"A watch repair shop."

Bev could picture it clearly, like it was last month (because it was): the dusty little shop with dark brown trim around the picture windows, brown and yellow striped awnings with "Tick

Tock Clock Shop" printed in script on them, the tidy sidewalk in front shaded by a maple (the street had been lined with them). It had been only a few blocks over from Pops's hardware store. Even here now with Conrad, a lump formed in Bev's throat and she felt a wave of nostalgia . . . or was that homesickness?

Conrad glanced at the now-lime green and hot orange striped awning as they went in under it. "I don't remember this ever being anything other than a frozen yogurt joint."

Bev mumbled some excuse that maybe she was thinking of somewhere else, but she got to thinking. Watch repair shop reminded her of the Fifties Chix—oh! She was supposed to meet up with them and go talk to Mr. F! She briefly considered squelching the realization . . . perhaps she could ask the girls' forgiveness later; they would understand. But she had remembered and she couldn't pretend she didn't.

She had stopped in the doorway.

"It can be a watch repair place if you want," teased Conrad.

"It's not that. I just remembered that I was supposed to meet my friends."

"Oh."

"No, really."

A couple came from the street, excusing themselves as the pushed past Bev. "Are you in line?" they asked Conrad who stood inside.

He raised his eyebrows at Bev. She shook her head no. "I guess not," Conrad said. Bev recognized that edge in his voice.

"I'm so sorry," Bev said as sincerely as she could. He probably had no idea just how sorry she was.

Or maybe he did, because he softened. "Do you need a ride?"

She nodded. "I need to go to my friend Mary's house."

On the way over, Bev found the courage to assure Conrad she hadn't wanted to cut their time together short and ask if she could see him again. Her belly did a flip flop when he agreed. When they arrived at Mary's, Bev thought the place looked unusually vacant. The little Victorian house showed no signs of life, and the driveway was empty. She wondered if her friends had left without her—in which case, she could feel justified in continuing her date with Conrad. She asked him to please wait while she dashed to Mary's front door.

She had barely rung the doorbell when Mary flung the door open and hurled herself on Bev, babbling, "You came! I should have known I could count on you! I called and no one was home and everyone else is gone and Aunt Row isn't well!"

"Whoa, slow down there, freckles. Don't have a cow! What's going on?" But Bev hugged her back. It felt nice to be needed, even by someone who was on the verge of hysteria.

Mary, near tears, composed herself and explained that Aunt Row wasn't well, James was with her, and their other friends had bailed on going to visit Mr. F. "But it's not just all that, Bev. Something feels very wrong, like we're stuck or we're missing something really big."

"Like what?"

"I just have a funny feeling that time is running out. We should be doing something *more*."

Bev suppressed a sigh. Just when she was going to ask if she could continue her date with Conrad, she could see that was not an option. Mary noticed Conrad in the car in the driveway. "Hey, isn't that Maxine's cousin . . . ?"

Bev blushed and Mary's eyes lit up with understanding. "Oh! Has this been going on—I mean, have you liked him—?"

"For a while," Bev said, smiling sheepishly.

"What will your parents think?" Mary said suddenly, in a scandalized whisper.

"You sound like you've already time traveled back to 1955! Look, should I send him away or what? There's no use in him sitting there while we gab on all day."

"Oh, no, don't send him away! See if he'll take us to Mr. F's. Otherwise, we don't have a ride."

Bev hesitated. Conrad wasn't in on the whole time travel thing and Bev didn't want to go weirdsville on him with that little detail of her life. She had just hoped it would be a bridge they would never have to cross. And now here it was looming. Mary saw her concern without Bev saying a word about it.

So Mary lowered her voice, even though Conrad sat in the car with the windows up to keep the AC in, and said, "He doesn't have to know the whole reason why we're going; I can be discreet—" she almost said, *I'm not Judy*, but stopped herself— "plus, you'll get to spend a little more time with him if he drives us."

Bev knew Mary was playing her like a fiddle with that last line, but she agreed.

Within moments, introductions were made, and Conrad agreed good-naturedly to take the girls to the Fairviews' house for "Mary's" school project. At first, Bev wasn't keen on sharing Conrad with Mary, but when Mary started asking about Conrad's family to make conversation as they drove across town to the far west part of the county, Bev was grateful to hear details she hadn't had the nerve to ask him about.

The girls learned that Conrad's parents were divorced (Mary offered her sincere condolences) and his mom and four sisters and a little brother lived in Louisiana with his aunt.

"Why didn't you go with your mother?" Mary asked. It wouldn't have occurred to her to live with her dad instead of her mom.

"I felt bad for my dad, I guess. She makes him feel like a nervous wreck; he works two jobs to pay child support. I just didn't want him to feel lonely."

"That's really sweet, Conrad," Mary said, taking the words that Bev didn't have the guts to say right out of her mouth. Conrad seemed uncharacteristically modest and Bev wanted to hug him.

Instead, Bev blurted, "Well, let's get ready for this meeting with Mr. F so we can make the most of it."

"Righto," said Mary, adjusting her glasses. She pulled out a notebook. "First and foremost, I think we'll want to ask him about Mrs. F's friend, that dancer, Emily Jackson."

Just then the car swerved abruptly and the girls threw their hands to the sides of the car to brace themselves.

"Sorry," Conrad apologized. "But did you just say Emily Jackson?"

"Yes," Mary said, trying to calm her heavily pounding heart.

"She's my aunt," he said. "What do you want to know?"

4

Poetry Slam

Maxine felt like a little kid and a grown-up all at the same time. She was thrilled her big sister had included her in the event at the coffeehouse—she had stars in her eyes—but she wanted to play it cool.

Mel's friend Lester drove to the coffeehouse and Maxine listened from the back seat to their conversation in the front of the car. They debated about the president; Lester argued that the African American president had been elected because of the color of his skin (and that it was a good thing), while Mel argued that it would only be a good thing if he proved to be a good president. Then they debated whether or not he was doing well so far. Just when Maxine was ready to agree with one over the other, a new opinion was set forth and she followed it in a new direction. Much of the recent political history the two referenced was over Maxine's head, even though she tried to pay attention in history class. Now she understood how everyone else felt who hadn't actually lived through certain aspects of history.

As she listened, she rested her hand possessively on the satchel on her lap. Maxine had done something risky: she'd sneaked the quill into her bag. She considered it her good luck charm and she wanted it near when she went up on stage. It was a valuable antique and a precious family heirloom marking her great-grandmother's freedom from slavery, so Maxine had made a vow to the universe that she would guard it with her life.

When they arrived at the coffeehouse, Maxine was disappointed. She'd imagined a subterranean dive with stone and cement walls, dim lighting flickering from red candles placed on wobbly round tables, around which huddled college-aged beatniks of all skin tones. The coffeehouse was the exact opposite: floor-to-ceiling windows on three sides allowed natural daylight to pour in, the tables' sleek and sturdy metal legs appeared to be bolted to the floor, and the modern decor seemed recently buffed and disinfected. Plush sofas and chairs lining the perimeter were covered in coordinating fabrics, not the threadbare, mismatched saggy furniture Maxine would have expected. The only thing that Maxine was pleased to see was the mixture of people: African American, Asian, Hispanic, and white students had gathered together, reminding Maxine of her own prediction in that fateful "Travel to Tomorrow" report about the desegregation of society.

A scruffy-bearded white guy a little older than Mel wore a saggy knit cap despite the outside temperature, an army green coat, and rainbow socks. He strummed a guitar and sang while some listened, others chatted quietly, and yet others worked away on their computers. Maxine's breath caught and her heart fluttered; this felt like home.

Mel glanced at her little sister and said with a smile, "What do you think?"

Maxine couldn't speak. She just nodded. She couldn't wait to tell the Fifties Chix about this place, or better yet, to bring them there. Maybe it was time to let go of the fifties diner and be firmly planted in the future—er, present. Ann could display her art here, Judy could perform a monologue . . . .

There weren't any chairs or low tables left, so Maxine, Melba, and Lester leaned against a tall table on the side of the staging area. By the scruffy-bearded guy's second song, the noise had died down and folks started to focus on him. Lester offered to get Maxine and Mel coffees. Mel asked for an iced soy chai latte because she wasn't "doing dairy," and Maxine said she wanted the same thing; but she had no idea what she'd just ordered. When Lester returned with their drinks, and Mel reached for her wallet to pay him back, he said not to worry about it; it was only eight dollars. Maxine was glad she wasn't sitting—she would have fallen off her chair. Coffee had been less than a dime in 1955!

An Asian girl in combat boots and a periwinkle tutu welcomed everyone and introduced two other girls; one played the flute and the other read a poem and sang parts of it. It was mostly off-key, but in a charming way. There were three individuals in a row, including Mel, who read poems. Maxine marveled at how strong and self-assured her big sister was. She captivated the room, filling the space with her rich voice, pulling back at quiet parts and booming at other parts. Maxine didn't understand the meaning behind most of her poem, but she could tell everyone else did. There were hearty nods and cries of "Oh, yeah," that reminded Maxine of church. No wonder this felt like a religious experience. She even liked the iced soy chai latte.

As the small crowd clapped and cheered for Mel, she returned to her spot next to Maxine, glowing and winded. "Ready? You're up next."

The room, which had before felt filled with warm light, now seemed blindingly bright. Maxine's stomach sank as if she were being pushed off a cliff and had just missed grabbing the edge. The thought of going onstage and reading one of her poems—let alone both—made her feel like she was going to lose consciousness. Mel must have known how to interpret Maxine's expression because she said, "Just take a deep breath. Everyone feels like you do before they go up there, but once you're there, you'll love it."

Maxine wanted to believe her, wanted her feet to move in the direction of the makeshift staging area, but she was as bolted to the floor as the tables were. Melba leaned in close to Maxine and whispered, "I double dog dare you." Maxine's eyes widened and she blinked back tears. Growing up, Maxine and Melba's favorite game had been daring and double dog daring each other to do things; Maxine was overcome with emotion at hearing that this phrase from what she thought was a bygone era was here and now.

She could do this; plus, it was officially no longer an option, now that she had been double dog dared. She gave Mel a grateful hug, reached into her bag, and retrieved her poems with a trembling hand. Approaching the stage, she fumbled with the paper, turning it right side up, but turning it one time too many. The crowd chuckled, but it was friendly and it put Maxine at ease. She turned the paper back and forth two more times just to get a laugh and suddenly the fear was gone. Confidence bloomed in her and she took in the moment consciously. She didn't remember when she'd ever quite felt so alive. *This must be what Bev feels like on the field, or Judy on the stage,* Maxine thought. She loved thinking of them right then, bringing them with her into this experience.

"Where I come from," Maxine started, reading the title. She paused dramatically and continued, taking her cue from Melba with pace and tone.

Where I come from, we don't leave the house at night.
Where I come from, we starve on a daily diet of fright.
Where I come from, the blacks eat and drink over there.
Where I come from, whites aren't concerned how we fare.
Where you are, nighttime is for slumber parties.
Where you are, the new hepcats are the smarties.
Where you are, we sit and eat together, unworried.
Where you are I now emerge with you from the past unhurried.

There was a pause that threatened to make Maxine nervous and then everyone burst into applause. She read her second poem, "Eternal Destiny," and reveled in the rush once again.

In fact, she was so high that when it was all over, she chatted and laughed with the people Melba introduced her to and got so full on the present, she entirely forgot her bag. And the quill that was in it.

In a panic as they approached the driveway, Maxine pleaded for Lester to take them back to the coffeehouse. She couldn't admit to Melba that the quill had been in the bag, only telling her that she'd left her purse. Maxine raced in to the room and searched everywhere, even asking the manager and the employees; but no one had seen her satchel. And no one had turned in a missing antique quill.

5

Attention, Please

Judy changed clothes twice and re-did her hair three times. She felt like she was auditioning today for Roger Streeter, instead of tomorrow for the summer school musical *110 in the Shade*. Her mom had been spending all her free time—and even her days at work—with Roger and Judy was feeling the pressure. She didn't even consider if she would like Roger, but she wanted him to approve of her so her mom could be proud.

She tried on her yellow pedal pushers and a white blouse. Did these pants make her look fat? Had she gained weight? She frowned. That would never do. She took the pants off and replaced them with a skirt. As she zipped the back of the light wool skirt, she thought of asking Mary for a new wardrobe and then had a peachy idea: Mary could do the costumes for the musical! Judy smiled and caught a glimpse of herself in the mirror. Hm. She did an experiment: frown. Smile. Frown. Smile. She looked like a different person when she smiled. She made a note to herself, remembering something she'd once heard: "I've never seen a smiling face that was not beautiful."

Judy jumped when she realized her mom was standing in the doorway. "You're perfect, do you know that?" Bitsy asked.

Judy blushed. "You're supposed to say that, you're my mom." But she was as filled with pleasure as if she'd just taken a gulp of hot chocolate filling her with sweet warmth. Judy hadn't felt seen by her mom in a long time and she tried to remember if she'd always felt that way, or only in the future.

"I am your mom and I love you, so of course I see you as perfect."

Judy watched from her vanity mirror as Bitsy leaned against the door frame. Judy still thought Bitsy was prettier than almost any of the Hollywood starlets on Judy's wall. She had bright eyes and a confidence and ease with which she carried herself, as if she were entirely unapologetic for taking up space. Judy realized that was what made her mother beautiful and she understood why her mom thought she was perfect. Because when you love people, you don't care about them more or less because of their size, shape, or color. Judy couldn't wait to tell Maxine what she'd realized. Isn't that what Maxine had been trying to say all along, since the day in the five-and-dime when they'd been getting sodas and planning their "Travel to Tomorrow" project together?

"You ready to meet Roger?" Bitsy asked.

Judy nodded. She was grateful Roger was coming to their place for lunch; and she was even more grateful her mom hadn't moved any of the pictures of Judy's dad from their place of honor in the living room. It was important that Roger see that both Judy and Bitsy still loved him.

Roger Streeter arrived only a few minutes later with sushi (which Judy was stunned to learn was *raw fish*), and Judy watched as her mom and Mr. Streeter hugged, nuzzled each other, and joked quietly as if they had known each other and been a couple forever. It was clear they had a world they inhabited together without Judy.

"Aren't you going to eat your sashimi?" Roger asked. They had gathered at the kitchen table, the bouquet of flowers he'd brought for Judy sitting in a vase in the middle. Bitsy had taken the flowers right from Judy's hand, thanked Roger, and put them in a vase. Judy had felt like they weren't for her after all. And now, as the three of them sat at lunch, Bitsy and Roger fed each other bites with chopsticks while Judy lost her appetite.

"Maybe she'd like a California roll," Bitsy suggested to Roger. "It's a little less daunting."

"You always know how to fix things," smiled Roger, touching Bitsy on the nose as if she were a baby or a kitten. Judy wanted to scream, *I'm right here!* But held her peace.

"How about it, Jujube; you want to try this one?" Bitsy tore her attention away from Roger long enough to offer Judy a shallow paper tray of what looked like rolls of rice cut into sections. Judy shook her head no, still unable to trust herself to speak civilly. Or without crying.

"What's wrong, sport? Are you not hungry?" Roger asked.

Sport? Judy thought with exasperation. *Do I look like a "sport" to you?*

"She thinks she needs to lose weight," Bitsy confided in her boyfriend.

"*Mother!*" Judy's face felt like it combusted into instant heat.

"Well, that's silly, sport. You're just as beautiful as your mom. Don't change a thing," Roger said cheerfully, totally ignoring Judy's obvious indignation.

"Mom! How dare you?" Judy protested.

"Honey, we're *family*; it's OK." Bitsy tried to soothe her daughter.

Judy jumped from her chair, knocking it backward; it teetered but didn't fall over, but the upset was enough to send the cats bounding out of the room in alarm. "We are not family," Judy managed to enunciate through her gritted teeth. "You two might be, but I'm nothing." She whirled around and stormed out of the kitchen. She thought she was headed for her room, but she found herself going as if on autopilot to the living room where her dad's pictures and medal were displayed.

She loaded up her arms with the frames.

"What in the world, Judy Elizabeth?" Her mother's mood had finally shifted to reflect Judy's and she stood with her hands on her hips watching Judy gather up the family's mementos.

"*He's* mine! You can have *yours*!" Her lip trembled and she steeled herself not to cry as she loaded the last picture on top of her heap—the picture of her dad with Judy on his shoulders as a laughing toddler.

Judy rushed to her room and realized she had to dump the frames on her bed before she could have a free hand to slam the door. Even then, the hollow door grazed the carpet and had a less than satisfying bang as it latched with a soft *click*. The most dramatic aspect of the slamming door was the gust of wind that that blew Judy's hair back and momentarily cooled her face as the hot tears began to course down her cheeks.

I want my dad, she thought to herself as she slid down the edge of her bed to the floor. She felt like a baby, but she didn't care. It wasn't fair. If she were going to time travel, why couldn't it be back in time so she could see her dad again and they could all be a family? She was frightened at how his memory was getting dimmer the older she got. She reached onto her nightstand and pulled her autograph book into her lap. She opened it and it naturally flopped to the place she always went first: the page with her dad's "autograph" and message to her. "Love Always," he'd written above his signature and next to the flower with a face he'd drawn.

Judy stared at the page through watery eyes, trying to divine a message behind his words since she couldn't have a conversation with him. She'd always thought he'd written "Love Always" as a message to her about how he'd always feel toward her, no matter what. But maybe he was sending her another message. Maybe he had meant to tell her to always love. (If that is what he'd meant, he'd never met slimy Roger Streeter, who was courting his wife and insulting his daughter. To add insult to injury, Roger was good-looking, polished, and successful. If only he'd been slovenly and unkempt.)

Judy sniffled and then gasped as, as if in slow motion, a fat wet tear fell from her face and splattered onto the page. Instantly, her dad's message lifted into the moisture from the paper and the ink swirled into marbleized ruin. "Nooo," moaned Judy, trying to blot it with her shirt and making it worse. A new sob escaped as her heart broke.

"Jujube?" Judy's mom's voice came from the other side of the door in a penitent murmur.

Judy closed her book, squeezing her eyes shut in denial. "What?" she replied after a delay.

"Can I please come in?"

"Where's Mr. Streeter?"

"He left," said Bitsy.

Judy agreed that she could come in. Bitsy opened the door gently and the two cats darted in before her. Dragnet hopped on the bed, ignoring the clutter and curling up on Judy's pillow, while Desi walked over Judy's legs and plopped down next to her knees and began licking his belly vigorously, as if he were trying to relieve stress. Bitsy sat on the other side of Judy so that Judy was now surrounded.

"That was really bad," Bitsy said. Judy, needless to say, was not in the mood to be reprimanded by her mom, but she was surprised when Bitsy continued, "I handled this whole thing terribly. I think I'm a better girlfriend than I am a mom."

Judy didn't disagree, but she felt a tinge of guilt starting to spread. Bitsy went on to explain that she had talked to Roger incessantly about Judy and felt like they all knew each other so well that meeting was just a formality.

"You might think he knows me because you talk about me all the time, but I never see you, so you never tell me about him. All I know is he's your boss and you like him."

"You're right. Ask me what you want to know about him."

For the next fifteen minutes, Judy pelted her mom with questions and learned that Roger had been married before, had two sons—a four-year-old and a six-year-old—and wanted to marry Bitsy and start a family together. Judy felt a stab of pain behind her eyes. She swallowed.

"And what do you want?" she asked her mom, not sure she wanted to hear the answer.

"I want you to love Roger as much as I do and then maybe I won't be reluctant to marry him."

Judy warmed to the idea of her mom being reluctant. Judy had no idea there could be the prospect of little brothers; the notion wasn't totally grody, it was just new information that would take a big adjustment.

"How much say do I have in this?" Judy asked, still grasping the autograph book so hard her hand was starting to hurt.

"When I said in the kitchen 'we're family,' I meant you and me," Bitsy said. "I'm not going to do anything that makes you miserable. I'm only considering marrying him because I think it would be wonderful for you to have a father figure again, and little brothers. And, of course," she added with a blush, "I *do* adore him."

Judy couldn't get into her mom's gushing about adoring Roger, but she did appreciate Bitsy's wanting to expand their family.

"We all know—Roger included—that he will never take the place of your dad," Bitsy said. "But that doesn't mean there still can't be a place for him. Love always makes room."

A fresh tear sprouted in Judy's eye as she was reminded her of ruined note from her dad . . . and another thought. Maybe her dad's sentiment had been incomplete. Maybe his contribution was love always and she needed to finish it by making room.

"OK, I'll give him another chance. But could you please try to cool it on the PDA?"

"Anything!" Bitsy squealed and Judy suddenly saw herself in her mom. Bitsy pulled out her phone. "He didn't really leave," she explained as she dialed. "He's sitting in his car in the driveway. He still wants to help you with your audition. He played Starbuck in "The Rainmaker" in college, you know . . . ."

He played Starbuck? Well, that explains everything, Judy thought.

"Rodge? Come on back in, honey. We both want to see you," said Bitsy excitedly into her phone.

Judy clutched her book to her chest, feeling further away from her dad than ever.

6

Family of Man

Ann Branislav had been surprised when Gary Jenkins had called her that morning. She'd been painting happily in the dining room, where she could look out the window at her dad's garden for inspiration. She wondered how Gary had gotten her number since her mom wasn't working for his mom as their maid these days. But she didn't wonder for long because Gary's manners had kicked in and he'd asked if it was all right that he'd called; he'd asked his mom for Kat's number.

"I hope you don't mind," he said.

Ann didn't mind at all, especially after the previous night, when they'd hung out at the diner together. Everyone around them had been laughing and talking and the two of them had gotten into a deep conversation. Gary was intelligent, funny, kind—and he had listened to her and showed genuine care about her thoughts and opinions. He even found her quirks— the things about her that came from her growing up in a 1950s orthodox Jewish setting—endearing. Ann loved Bev, but Gary was poles apart from his little sister in many ways. As she had fallen asleep last night, Ann had even considered confiding in Gary about their time travel adventure; but she didn't want a distraction from their budding friendship.

"I was just wondering if you'd like to go to the library with me today," Gary asked now on the phone.

"I thought you had that paper due," Ann laughed.

"That's why I need to go to the library! And I thought you could come with me and help out if I get stuck."

"I told you all I know about Belgrade," said Ann. She thought it was an amazing coincidence that he was writing a paper about the Balkans, of all places, for his AP World History final. When she could get up the nerve, she would ask if he'd chosen the topic because of her.

Suddenly Ann realized that meeting Gary at the library might not even be an option; she had no idea how her parents would feel about her seeing a gentile boy. Surely in 1955, it would not have been an option. Her heart sank. The thought of lying to her parents and telling them she'd be meeting her friends crossed her mind; she'd be seeing them later in the day anyway, so it wouldn't be a total lie. But no matter what she thought of her parents' perceived laxity in observing their faith, it wasn't license for her to abandon her principles and be knowingly dishonest. She asked Gary if he'd mind waiting while she checked with her parents.

Sheepishly, Ann approached her mom, who was on the computer as always, doing bookkeeping for the cleaning business she owned with Gary's mom.

"You can say no, certainly, but can I ask your permission for something?"

"Of course," Kat said without looking up or pausing.

"Gary, uh, Gary *Jenkins*, that is, asked if I would accompany him to the library—"

"Oh, Gary? He's fabulous! Go and have fun."

Ann returned to the phone and accepted Gary's invitation. Naturally, Ann looked forward to spending a little more time with Gary, but she was confounded by her mom's easy acceptance of Ann going out with him.

"Where's Tatty?" Ann asked. Maybe her dad would have something to say about her going out with a Christian boy.

"How sweet; I haven't heard you call your dad that in years." Kat smiled. She kept tapping away on the keyboard. "He's taken Alex to meet with Rabbi Rivkin."

"Rabbi Rivkin?" Ann's spirits lifted. The rabbi was orthodox; that had to be a good sign. "Well, I hope it goes swell. I'll be home before dinner."

"OK, sweetheart." Kat blew her daughter a kiss and kept working.

Ann had just finished cleaning up her paints in the dining room when Gary came to pick her up. She went to wash her hands and overheard her mother chatting happily with Gary.

"Your mom's great. I'm glad she and my mom are working together. I really think they'll make a go of it," Gary said as they drove away in his car. Ann thought of how different things had been in 1955, when Mrs. Jenkins had been her mom's boss, not partner. "Hey, I have a surprise for you before we go to the library."

Ann glanced at Gary and smiled. He looked scrubbed clean—not that he ever looked less than clean—and the sharp scent of cologne or aftershave stung her nose and made her eyes water.

He was trying very hard to impress her and she found herself shifting in her seat uncomfortably. She was only just getting to know him. Was he considering this a date?

When they got on the highway to head to the city, she had to say something. What had happened to going to the library, which was only a couple miles away? Ann realized she hadn't been on the highway since they had arrived in the future. Cars jammed the roadway, all speeding and zipping around. Some were tall, like trucks all covered over with metal, while others were tiny compared to the blue plymouth her tatty had used to drive in 1955.

"We will still go to the library, but I thought we could go to the one in the city. But there's a stop I wanted to make before that, on our way. I think you'll like it," Gary assured her.

It didn't seem that Ann had much of a choice.

After passing a couple more exits, Gary turned the car up an off-ramp, drove a few blocks, and turned into the main entrance of the university campus.

Gary parked in a large student parking lot which gleamed with cars like hard-shelled insects sunning themselves on a big patio. They entered the nearest building with tall tinted windows and were met with a blast of dry, icy air conditioning. Ann shivered and Gary asked if she was OK. She appreciated how attentive he was.

They passed a small booth that was closed and Gary said, "It's free on Sunday."

She was about to ask what was when they passed through a set of heavy smooth maple double doors into a huge expansive gallery. The overhead lights were dim, but the paintings, photographs, charcoal drawings, and occasional metal sculpture lining the walls each had their own individual spots, like pinpricks in the ceiling allowed the sun to flood right on them. Ann sucked in her breath; how thoughtful of Gary to take her to an art showing—and then she began to realize what the theme of the show was.

"It's a touring show of Holocaust art," Gary explained in hushed tones. "If you've already seen it, or aren't interested, we can go. I just didn't have anyone to see it with myself and thought you might—"

Ann couldn't speak, so she just nodded vigorously yes. Gary handed her a program that he'd picked up on the way in and kept one for himself, but neither of them looked at the paper in their hands. They started at the first painting and slowly worked their way around the room. Neither of them said a word, but at one painting, they instinctively grabbed hands and didn't let go.

The painting, in tones of gray and sepia, was of a family: grandparents, children, parents, brothers, sisters. It wasn't a formal portrait where they all stood together in rows, but vignettes of the individuals, as if the painting were composed of memories or prophecies or both. The people weren't emaciated, like some of the victims depicted in the other art; but their eyes were haunted, intelligent. As Ann studied it, she realized that the individuals were paired off—a son and father, a grandfather and baby, and mother and daughter—and each pair was embracing. It was either the beginning of the Holocaust for them, Ann surmised, with their softness not yet hardened to the harsh lines of abuse and deprivation, or subsequent generations reliving the memories of a horrific past that could not be absolved. As was her habit, she studied the painting before reading the description or artist's name.

When at last her eyes drifted to the sign next to the piece, she caught her breath and a funny sound escaped.

Family of Man, by N. Brajer. Sajmište Concentration Camp, outskirts of Belgrade (now Serbia), Dec. 1941. The depiction is the artist's response to being interned at the Jewish ghetto which contained 40,000 prisoners, made up of Jews and Gypsies who were determined by Nazis to be "informants for the rebels." By May 1942, 14,500 of the 16,000 Jews in Serbia had been murdered. Perhaps the artist was predicting a shift from a legacy that included progeny extending into future generations to a depiction of generations never to be.

It was then that Ann and Gary grasped hands. Gary must have known that the artist's name, *Brajer,* was a family name on Ann's mother's side; after all, it was Ann's cousin's last name, and Gary had spent the last couple days emailing her for hours at a time.

"Do you think that could be—"

"Your great-grandmother?" Gary whispered. Ann didn't correct him that it was her grandmother, only a generation removed, not two. It would have opened a whole other conversation that she wasn't ready to have, about how her parents had actually emigrated to America in 1937 and how she had been born just a year before this painting had been made and her grandmother killed.

"Did you know? Is that why you brought me here?" she asked.

Gary's eyes were wide with wonder. "No, I had no idea. I just saw what the show was about and thought of you. What was her name?" Gary asked.

"Nikka Brajer."

"*N. Brajer.* We need to find out from the curator who 'N. Brajer' is and what info they have about her. What are the chances there would be an N. Brajer who's a Jewish Serbian artist and *not* related to you?"

"She was originally from Russia, but yes, I was thinking the same thing."

Hands still clasped, they proceeded to the front of the exhibit.

Going to the exhibit and talking to the curator took them longer than Ann had expected. She had missed going with her friends to see Mr. F and hoped they would forgive her. Maybe she could still catch the end of the meeting, but first, it was time to talk to Gary.

"I think I have to tell you something," Ann said as they drove in an awkward silence. Her voice came out high and squeaky and she cleared her throat. She knew she had acted oddly when they had spoken with the curator, being vague about her possible (probable) relation to the artist because of the questionable timetable, and she hoped Gary attributed her behavior to shock and bewilderment. Which was accurate, but for more reasons than he knew.

Gary seemed pleased that she was about to confide in him and Ann was heartened. "The 'N. Brajer' could be my grandmother. Not my great-grandmother, but my grandmother. My parents," she cleared her throat again. This wasn't going well; she should have organized her thoughts better. "They actually left Yugoslavia—"

"Serbia?"

"No, I do mean Yugoslavia. They emigrated to the States in 1937 just before Hitler came in."

Ann paused, not to wait for commentary or start a conversation, but to collect her thoughts. Gary's confused expression shifted to amusement, and Ann preferred confused because *amused* meant he thought she was joking around. "Mrs. F was Miss Boggs before she got married in 1955. Miss Boggs was my social studies teacher and she gave four other students and me a group assignment to predict life 55 years into the future. The day after the assignment the five of us woke in that future—your present day."

Gary chuckled, but it was forced.

"I know it sounds crazy, but it's been even crazier living it."

"Oh, I bet," his fake grin continued. "So how old are you really?"

"I'm fifteen. I'm serious, Gary."

"I can see that you're serious. You should lighten up, it's a great story."

A pause in conversation made the turn signal Gary flipped on to turn left seem exceptionally loud.

"I guess you don't have to believe me—"

"So, you are time traveling? Or are you visiting a parallel universe?" Gary's tone indicated that he wasn't asking a sincere question.

Ann wished she hadn't mentioned it. It had felt like an impulsion, but now she desperately wished she'd had the restraint to keep her mouth shut. "I shouldn't have brought it up."

After a strained interlude and as they pulled up to Ann's house, Gary said quietly, "If you don't like me or don't want to hang out, I wish you had just said that instead of making up some ridiculous scenario. I've been shot down before, but this takes the cake."

The car stopped in front of Ann's house. "I was born in 1940, I'm fifteen years old and I don't know if we time traveled, are visiting a parallel universe, or what. But Miss Boggs—now Mrs. Fairview—has aged while no one else has. I really like you—at least what I know of you—but if this is too weirdsville for you, I understand. But please don't tell anyone. And . . . thank you for today."

Ann climbed out of the car, trudged up to her house, and was sad but not surprised when Gary drove away once she was inside. Holding back tears, she went to the first thing that could comfort her and the first thing she wanted to touch in her hands after the art exhibit.

"Mom!" she called from the dining room. Her paints and canvas were missing.

"Sorry, darling. Your painting supplies are in your room. You know me, always straightening. How was your time with Gary?" Kat said from the laundry room off the kitchen.

"Fine." Ann cut her answer short and raced to her room. Her door was open. She gasped; it was as if she'd seen it in her mind's eye before she actually saw it . . . and there it was: Meshuga on the floor with a nub of a paintbrush in his paws.

7

The Breach

"Your aunt?" Mary gasped, composing herself. Conrad had straightened the car, but Mary still had a roller coaster sensation of being jerked back and forth. "Is she the lady that's friends with Mrs. F?"

Conrad furrowed his brow. "I don't know about that. She lives in New Orleans and has for as long as I can remember."

Mary felt chills prickle all over her body. She cracked her window to let a little warm outside air flow in. "Maybe it's a different Emily Jackson," Mary said. But for some reason, she didn't think so. "I'm sorry to sound so gauche, but how old is she?"

Conrad laughed and reasoned, "She's my mom's younger sister, so I dunno, she's like 25 or 30?"

Mary's face screwed up, trying to work out the math as Conrad directed the car up a steep incline and they went through a forest to the top of a ridge and took a right, driving along the ridge line. It was a beautiful view of farmland, a small airport, and encroaching retail strip centers surrounded by slabs of parking lots. If there was anything that stood out about the future, it was the slabs of parking lots. The space where Jenkins Hardware used to be was now asphalt and the spaces were never close to being even half filled. Seemed like a waste of space.

"Which river is that?" wondered Bev out loud, putting aside the Emily Jackson mystery for the moment. Beyond the retail buildings, parking lots, and corn fields, a silver ribbon of water wound through another layer of bluffs.

"Missouri," Conrad said.

They passed three more mailboxes, and Mary said, "This must be it!"

Conrad turned the car in and they proceeded down a curvy tree-lined driveway to a circle drive. Mary's mental image of Mrs. F's house had been nothing like the mini mansion that appeared out of a cluster of trees at the base of the drive. It was lovely, to be sure, but it was more formal than Mary would have thought. The light brown two-story house sat on a spacious, well-landscaped, and formal plot that was unlike Aunt Row's cottage garden, crammed haphazardly with every kind of flower, tree, and shrub clamoring over each other for attention.

"Is he home?" Bev asked, feeling like she needed to speak in hushed tones.

"I hope so," Mary replied.

Conrad parked the car near a fountain. "Who knew Mrs. F was loaded?" Conrad said, echoing what the girls were thinking but didn't think was appropriate to say out loud.

Mary's heart pounded overtime as they rang the doorbell. She almost apologized to Conrad and Bev, certain that it was a loud distraction.

Mr. Fairview opened one of the heavily carved dark wood double doors. A paunchy, friendly-faced older man with a head of gunmetal gray hair, he apologized that they would have to reschedule since his wife was with an ill friend.

"Mr. Fairview," Mary insisted. "We just came to talk to you. We know she's at Row's house; I was there earlier. Might we please just have a minute of your time?"

"Ah, well, not sure what help I can be." Mr. F suddenly looked uncomfortable.

"We just need some fun facts or pictures or stuff like that for her surprise retirement assembly at school," Bev said.

Reluctantly, Mr. F let them in. As the double doors opened, a panorama of the valley through the back wall of windows came into view. A sunken living room was saturated with light and every dust-free, gleaming surface boasted an expensive, taste-fully placed artifact or antique. This was more like what Mary would have expected; she just bet every one of those things had a story behind it. So very unlike the sparse and vacant apartment above Aunt Row's garage that Mrs. F retreated to on occasion to be closer to work—and to Aunt Row, Mary now presumed.

Mary couldn't help herself; she immediately baited Mr. F. "Sure looks like you or Mrs. F do a lot of traveling."

He glanced around as he ushered them right past the living room to the formal dining room. "Indeed," he answered simply.

Mary had hoped they could settle in in the living room; she liked the view. The dining room was dark with heavily-leaded windows draped with heavy silk curtains and weighed down by tassels. Now she was really wondering if she knew Mrs. F at all. This was not the kind of decor Mary would have attributed to her favorite teacher.

"We don't use this room very much, but I thought it might be nice to keep the sun out of our eyes and—Helga?—enjoy some snacks."

A thin, pale, timid woman appeared at the archway from the formal dining room to the butler's pantry. She wore a white blouse and khaki pants and her hair was in a frizzy, beige-colored bun.

"Helga, would you be so kind as to bring us some fruit punch and cookies?" Mr. F asked.

Bev and Mary arched their eyebrows at each other. Mrs. F had a maid? They were learning more about her every moment. The dining room table was a twelve foot long oval and Conrad, Bev, and Mary sat at one end while Mr. F sat a seat away around the softened corner. Mary pulled out her notebook and cleared her throat.

"We've got a few things—"

"Well, now, shouldn't we start with some introductions?" Mr. F smiled.

"Of course," Mary blushed. "Where are my manners? This is Beverly Jenkins and Conrad Marshall, and I'm Mary Donovan, the one you talked to about our coming over."

"I had gathered there were five of you—girls," said Mr. F.

"There were, but a few of us had commitments we couldn't get out of," Mary responded, quite proud of her diplomacy. She was still rather peeved that everyone except Bev had something better to do. "Conrad was kind enough to drive us."

He turned his attention to Conrad. "Marshall, huh? I believe I've got a Marshall working for one of my companies; Stitson HVAC. That your dad?"

"No, sir, that would be my uncle," Conrad said.

Mary was beginning to get antsy. She had a lot of questions for Mr. F. If Aunt Row, Twig, and Mrs. F weren't going to help, she hoped Mr. F could offer some sort of missing puzzle piece.

"Such a small world," Mary said. "Speaking of small world, we just discovered that Conrad's aunt is a good friend of Mrs. F's." Bev's knee slammed into Mary's. Why hadn't she laid some sort of foundation or built up to it somehow?

"Is that right? Who would that be?" asked Mr. F.

"Emily Jackson," Conrad offered doubtfully. He'd said in the car he didn't know how Mrs. F and Aunt Em could be friends; his aunt had lived in New Orleans for as long as he could remember.

"Hm, doesn't ring a bell," said Mr. F. *But maybe it did ring a bell*, thought Mary. She'd seen something flicker in his eyes.

"They went to school together," Mary prompted.

Conrad laughed. "I doubt that, my aunt is not that—" he stopped himself from saying *old* and amended "—generation."

"There you have it. They couldn't have gone to school together," maintained Mr. F. Mary wondered why Mr. F was so quick to argue about it, but she was also trying to do the math. She'd been convinced they'd found their Emily in Conrad's aunt. But it just didn't work that she was their parents' age *and* a classmate of Mrs F's. Yet there had to be a—well, a *breach* of some kind somewhere. Mrs. F, her husband, Twig, and Row had all aged while the Fifties Chix and their families had not. Maybe Emily Jackson was somehow a link between the two dimensions! Now Mary really wanted to find Emily and see if Mrs. F's friend and Conrad's aunt were in fact the same person.

In the mean time, Helga had returned with tray containing a plate of cookies, fruit punch, and glasses.

"Do you have any funny stories about Mrs. F? Maybe when she first started teaching?" Mary changed the subject. She didn't want to get kicked out just yet.

"I don't know about funny stories, but she was always so passionate about her work. She loves history, loves her students. She's always designed creative assignments to get her students to learn something new."

Bev snorted then sheepishly apologized.

"Is there anything else, Helga?" Mr. F interrupted himself to ask the maid who was lingering nearby.

"Just wanted to make sure you had what you needed. Will you be wanting me to retrieve the clippings you set aside?"

"Of course!" Mr. F slapped his hand down on the table. "Where would I be without you? Please, bring them in."

She scuttled out of the room and returned less than a minute later with some newspaper clippings.

"Thought you might find these interesting," Mr. F said after thanking the housekeeper. He laid the papers in front of Mary and Bev.

Mary caught her breath and her eyes filled with tears. There was Mrs. F just as she'd remembered her: cat-eye glasses, curled and shellacked chestnut hair. And standing next to her was a young, 1955 Aunt Row, Mary realized. Her memory shot back to that Christmas dinner at her church where she'd seen James waiting on so many women; one of them had been a pretty lady on crutches. Mary was staring at that lady now in the social pages. Seeing Mrs. F in 1955 felt like home, and seeing young Aunt Row when Mary knew she wasn't well made Mary's heart ache.

Bev studied another picture. "What's the FairView Project?" she asked. Mary tore her eyes away and looked at Bev's clipping. It was another image taken from the social pages, this one a gala event for the FairView Project launch. Row wasn't in this one, but Mr. and Mrs. F were, and there was a man in the background of the picture that she was trying to place.

Mr. Fairview waved his hand nonchalantly. "One of my businesses. I've had my hand in a lot of things over the years. Marion —Mrs. Fairview—has always been so supportive of my various ventures."

Mary almost screamed, "Twig!" when she realized who the man in the photo reminded her of. Instead, with her mouth dry, she said, "Is it all right if we borrow these pictures for our presentation?"

Mr. F agreed and Mary sensed their time together was coming to a close. She refocused her energy and asked Mr. F some questions, but she realized how trite they were. The answers might be useful for a tribute, but would not help her and Bev get any closer to the truth the Fifties Chix sought.

With warmth and pride, Mr. F gushed about his wife's commitment to her students, how she'd miss them so when she retired, and how he'd be glad to have her to himself for once.

Not long after, they said their thank yous and goodbyes and Conrad, Mary, and Bev traipsed to the car. Mary's stomach felt like a hard knot of disappointment: she was still feeling let down by the three friends who hadn't accompanied them, and she was dissatisfied with the visit. She also felt secretly embarrassed. Had she thought Mr. F would come out and say his wife had a penchant for time travel and made other people do it, too? All she had was more questions. Primarily, what had Twig been doing at a gala with the Fairviews? It could have been a coincidence, but Mary was kicking herself for not simply asking Mr. F if it was Twig and if so, what he'd been doing there.

Mary closed the back door of Conrad's car and they were about to back out when Conrad slammed on the brakes and the car lurched.

"What in the—?"

Conrad rolled down Mary's window with the push of a button.

Helga, out of breath, said, "Sorry, I didn't want to miss you. I think you left your pen."

"Gosh, I didn't—" But Mary took the pen Helga passed her, even though she hadn't left anything behind.

"Have a nice evening," Helga said before walking briskly back to the house.

"What was that about?" Bev said. "How kooky. You didn't leave a pen, did you, freckles?"

"No," Mary said. But she looked at the little scrap of paper wrapped around the pen Helga had handed her: *I might have something you need to see*—and Helga had scrawled a phone number. "She had a message for me, I guess." Mary's mind whirled. "Bev, she knows something! I think this could be our big break!"

8

Big Break

The auditorium was dark and freezing, and Judy found herself shivering in the back row. She hadn't been nervous until the goosebumps had popped up all along her arms, and then she confused the chills with anxiety.

Students were scattered around the room as the director instructed them on the procedure for auditioning. She'd put her name in and after being addressed, they were to exit to the hallway and wait to be called in. Judy didn't much like the idea of hanging out with the competition in broad daylight in the lobby, but she hoped at least it would be a bit warmer and she could calm her clattering nerves.

Last night, after Roger had come back into the house, Judy had been on her best behavior. Admittedly, it was partly because he had played Starbuck, the male lead in the play that the musical "110 in the Shade" was based on. But Judy could also surmise that if she were ever to feel closer to her mother again, she'd have to show some sort of enthusiasm for her mom's real-life "Starbuck."

Roger must have had the same insight as Judy: if he wanted to get closer to her mother, he'd have to show some enthusiasm for Judy. He'd coached her on her two monologues and one song, and given her some insight into the character "Lizzie," for whom she was auditioning.

"You are sweet and bubbly and bright, so you'll have to find a darker side," Roger said, working compliments into his advice whenever he could. Judy almost said, *You'd be surprised,* thinking of how she'd "befriended" Diane Dunkelman to spy on her.

Now in the hallway, waiting for her name to be called and forcing herself to relax and breathe, Judy focused on her dad. It was Memorial Day, appropriately enough, and she planned on a perfect audition that she'd feel proud to dedicate to him. Letting Roger help her was a favor Judy had done for her mom, but her performance today was for her dad.

And maybe for Bob Jenkins a little, too.

"OMG, this is the cutest!" Judy heard a high-pitched familiar syrupy voice behind her. "Are you *auditioning*?"

Judy's nerves took up their jumpiness again as she whipped around to find herself face to face with Diane Dunkelman. *When is this chick going to be held accountable for hurting Maxine?* Judy thought. Diane had set up a fake page online, attributed it to Maxine, and then had "Maxine" threaten to bring a gun to school. While the incident was being investigated, Diane had played in a softball tournament over the weekend with Bev.

Diane must have read Judy's mind because she said, "Chill out. I'm not auditioning. I'm just here with her." She gestured carelessly toward her friend, Katie.

"Hi," Katie said.

"Hi," Judy said, regretting not asking any of her friends to accompany her. It hadn't occurred to her that she'd have to confront Diane Dunkelman today. They had the day off in observance of Memorial Day, and one of the many perks of not being in class was not having to deal with Diane. But Saturday night they had ended up at the same diner, Judy on one side of Bob Jenkins and Diane on the other. Judy hadn't liked competing for Bob's attention, and now she didn't like the thought of dividing her attention between the audition and Diane.

Feeling like a coward but certain that she had no other choice but to take leave of Diane, Judy excused herself to the restroom. Once there, she came across four other girls who were probably avoiding Diane as well. They looked as unsettled as Judy felt. Her heart went out to them.

Taking her cue from Diane, Judy did the opposite and asked with genuine interest if they were there to audition. When they said yes, she told them she was sure they would do great. "My mom's boyfriend gave me some great advice. He played Starbuck in college. He said when you're auditioning, you shouldn't pretend like you're alone practicing in front of the mirror; you should pretend it's opening night and the house is packed. He said it's harder to act for a small crowd than a big one."

"That's true," one girl said, visibly relaxing.

They all chatted a few more minutes and after more well wishes, Judy turned to go.

"Did you forget why you came in here?" the girl said. "Don't you need to use the bathroom?"

"No, I was just avoiding Diane Dunkelman," said Judy and the girls laughed.

Judy came back to the main lobby in time for her name to be called. As she walked up the long, darkened aisle to the stage, her heart pounding in that invigorating way as if she had just spotted Bob across the room, she wondered if she should have given advice to the girls—her competition—in the restroom. As she climbed the stairs to the stage, she decided yes. It felt good to help someone else, even just a little, and she realized it had calmed her nerves.

As directed, she stated her name, and before she started her first monologue, she eyeballed Diane sneaking in the back auditorium door. Judy wanted to tell the director and the two other teachers on either side that there was an intruder, but she didn't want to be a tattle-tale. That couldn't bode well for her audition, even if they did kick Diane out. Instead, Judy imagined the theater sold out, standing room only, with Diane in the back of the room and Bob in the front row, flanked by her best friends—the Fifties Chix.

Judy knew she was pulling off the perfect audition when Diane got up in the middle of Judy's song and loudly exited the auditorium, letting the door slam behind her. Judy took the joy that welled up in her and churned it into new energy, finishing the song on a strong note.

"*Very* nice, Judy. Thank you," the director said from a dimly lit spot beyond Judy's line of sight.

Judy grinned and skipped off the stage. She knew she should have stayed in character, but she couldn't help it. She was confident that she'd earned herself a callback.

For the second morning in a row, Mary found herself wondering how early was too early to make a call. She had Helga's number on top of her sewing machine—the best place she could think to put such an important item—and she stared at it while she lay in bed as the sun crept up over the horizon behind a thick veil of clouds.

She hadn't heard from James last night, and she wished that he and the Fifties Chix could have been at the Fairviews' house. She was also worried about Aunt Row, but didn't want to intrude on the family by pestering James for updates. The only thing she could do was pray. Usually that was a great comfort, but this morning she had a hard time getting her thoughts in order and an even harder time trusting, which she knew was an essential ingredient.

She heaved a sigh and climbed out of bed. Whatever mysteries she had yet to solve, there was one thing she knew: she had committed to helping out with Mrs. F's tribute and she'd started that quilt. She didn't have to act like a deer in headlights when there was plenty she knew she could be doing. She took Helga's scrap of paper, deciding to put it in her diary for safekeeping.

But her diary was not in its normal hiding place. This had happened periodically and she'd left notes to her siblings in the pages of her diary to stop reading it just in case, but now her suspicions were confirmed. When she discovered her diary upside down under her bed, her throat felt raw with dread. She pulled the little book out and saw ink and finger print smudges on the cover; inside, marker scribbles of all colors filled the pages.

"No!" Mary cried and held her diary to her chest. As she bowed her head, something caught her eye that she hadn't noticed last night before bed. The cover on her Singer Featherweight didn't look right. Gasping again, she sprang to the sewing machine and inspected the cover, lifting it off. To her horror, someone had tried to "sew" clay; the needle was jammed and the sewing feet were glopped with multi-colored pasty dough. The needle had gone down into the bobbin well, spreading the clay into the inner workings of the sewing machine.

Rage and disbelief blurred Mary's vision. "Who did this?" she screamed, not caring who was still sleeping. "Who did this?" She ran out of her room as her grandmother appeared from her bedroom at the base of the stairs.

"Mary," she demanded, hoping Mary wouldn't wake the younger kids. "Please, hush."

"I will not hush, Nana! Some little monster destroyed my sewing machine! Danny, I know it was you!" she screeched down the hall toward her brother's room.

Now Mary's mother's door flung open. "What in the world —? Mary, please."

"Don't 'Mary, please' me! Those ankle biters are out of control! Have they ever been told no in their short pitiful lives? It's amazing that they haven't because I get told no—"

"Mary!" Her mom and grandma yelled in unison.

"—*every day of my life!*"

Now her sisters were standing at their bedroom door and Danny was wailing behind his.

Through clenched teeth, Mary's mom approached her, hissed, "Downstairs. Now," and steered Mary toward the stairwell.

Mary shook as she made her way down the stairs, barely able to make it without stumbling. She would not cry, she would not cry; she was too angry, she told herself. But by the bottom step, tears were burning her eyes.

Once in the kitchen, Mary's mom started in. "We do not talk like that in this house."

"Well, maybe we should start! Those kids run wild and they ruined my sewing machine. That sewing machine is my life! It represents everything dear to me."

"Just what does it represent?" Nana asked. For once, she didn't head to the kitchen on autopilot to make coffee, but sat at the kitchen table with Mary and Mary's mom.

"Family," Mary said, not registering the irony until after she'd spoken the word.

"If family is so dear to you, why are you never home? Why have you made dinner for us just once in over a month, and why do you insist on treating your sisters and brother like undesirable nuisances?" Mary's mom challenged.

Mary resented the tone and her mother's approach. She hadn't had her mother's attention in months and now she did—as if she were the criminal.

"Let her be, Jane," Nana said. "She's a teenager."

"A teenager that needs a talking to," Mary's mom said.

Mary's tears had dried up, maybe because her cheeks were so hot they instantly scorched the tears into nonexistence. "I'm going through a hard time right now," Mary piped up.

"Yeah. She time traveled."

Mary, her mom, and Nana spun in their seats to see one of the twins, Patty, standing in the doorway to the kitchen in her pajamas.

"Patty!" Mary exclaimed. She could tell by the way Patty looked at her that Patty believed Mary had time traveled. "I was —I was writing a story. It's private!"

"I know. That's why I scribbled in it, so you would think it was Danny. Please don't be mad." She burst into tears. *Oh, brother.* Mary knew *that* trick.

"Come here, pumpkin," Mary's mother soothed, reaching for Patty.

Mary's mouth dropped open. Was her mom really comforting Patty for ruining Mary's life just because she shed a few tears? "Nana!" Mary protested, searching for an ally.

"Patty, please apologize," Nana said gently.

Mary was stunned. Of all the parallel universes, this was the kookiest. She stood up and the three others in the room paused to look at her. "I have to go," she said.

"Sit down, honey, we'll work this out."

"No. I can't be here right now." She'd never felt so clear. Every muscle and bone in her body and every thought in her head directed her to the front door. It wasn't a choice.

Unfortunately, as she stormed out the front door, rain fell all around her, she was still in her pajamas and robe, she'd left Helga's number in her room . . . and she had no idea where to go.

9

One Place, One Accord

It was stupid; she knew it was stupid. Yet Bev had tossed and turned all night, unable to sleep—and when she had managed to doze off, she was plagued by nonsensical dreams. If she was going to dream, she'd prefer to dream about Conrad like she had a couple nights before. But these restless, bizarre dreams made her more tense and exhausted. They all revolved around her missing bat. And that's what she thought was stupid.

After she and Conrad had dropped Mary off at Mary's house, Bev had realized she'd left her bat at the park. She'd had her hat, mitt, and ball, but her bat was nowhere to be found in Conrad's car. She knew he must have thought she was overreacting when she'd begged him, in a near panic, to go back to the park to look for it. It was just a plain old wooden bat. But there was no way that she could explain that it had traveled with her from 1955 and was, she worried, her link back there. Not that she was sure about wanting to go back; but the thought of not even having the option was frightening.

They'd searched every inch of the park, even places they hadn't been close to, including a dumpster at the far end of the parking lot. As the sun was setting, Bev's head had been pounding. She had been getting snippy with Conrad and neither one of them liked that.

Giving up at last, she'd asked him to take her home. She'd been so disturbed, she almost hadn't noticed how patient Conrad was being with her: "I'll see if I can borrow Dad's car again tomorrow and since we don't have school, I'll come pick you up and we can look for it again." Bev did notice that he hadn't asked what the big deal about the bat was, and she was grateful.

So now, with thunder rumbling in the distance and rain starting to fall, Bev thought of her poor bat somewhere outside getting soaked, as if it were a precious pet lost far from home.

Bev knew it was more than just the bat; an uneasiness had settled in her bones. Even as she was thrilled to be spending time with Conrad off the field, she kept hearing Mary's words from the previous afternoon replay in her mind: *I just have a funny feeling that time is running out. We should be doing something more.*

All right, then. Despite being wiped out, Bev got up and stretched. She would go to Mary's so together they could call that Helga lady about the weird note she'd given Mary. Bev decided she would drag the rest of the Fifties Chix—kicking and screaming, if necessary—to a group meeting. Though Mary's idea of fun might be putting together a tribute for Mrs. F, it wasn't Bev's; yet it needed to be done. Funny how Bev's world had opened up when softball and baseball season had ended.

Leaving her room for the bathroom, Bev heard knocking—gently at first, and then increasing in volume and intensity. Her brothers were still sleeping, except for maybe Gary, who probably was pulling an all-nighter to write that paper. Bev crept down the stairs and looked out the peephole in the front door. Even now she wasn't used to answering the door herself; that had always been the charge of the housekeeper, Mrs. B.

Bev stifled a gasp at the sight on her front doorstep. She knew Mary couldn't have been aiming for comedy; it must have been an emergency for Mary to go out in robe and pajamas. There she stood, drenched to the bone, looking like a drowned, red-headed rat. Bev composed herself and opened the door. She expected Mary to leap inside, but instead, Mary looked at Bev through her rain-speckled glasses. Now Bev couldn't help the snort that escaped.

"It's not—"

"Funny; I know, I know. I'm sorry. Come in and tell me about it." Now Bev wished Mrs. B had been around. She would have retrieved some fluffy towels and put some tea on. Bev wasn't inclined to that sort of thing, but at least she'd thought of it. She could try it even if Mrs. B wasn't around.

Bev guided Mary to the laundry room off the kitchen and rifled through a pile of clean towels. Finding a big towel with her monogram on it, Bev handed it to Mary. Then she thought better of it. Snatching it back, she wrapped it around Mary's shoulders and vigorously rubbed Mary's arms.

"That's swell, Bev, but I'm not cold, just wet."

"Sorry. Come in the kitchen and we'll make you some tea. Even though you're not cold."

"Tea would be perfect," Mary agreed.

While Bev put the kettle on and emptied the dishwasher, she asked Mary the reason for her unexpected, early morning visit.

"I just had to get out of my house. I don't know who those people are anymore. I like lots of things about the future, but I miss lots of things about the past, too."

Bev could relate to that.

"And," Mary heaved a dramatic sigh, "I stormed out of my house, leaving the note from Helga."

Bev paused putting the spoons in their slot in the drawer and concentrated. She rattled off a phone number.

"Is that it?" Mary asked excitedly.

"I think so. I looked at that note yesterday and I'm not a math whiz, but I'm good with numbers if I can translate them to baseball stats."

The kettle whistled and Bev poured the steaming water into two mugs with tea bags. Bev wasn't one for tea, but she didn't want Mary to drink alone. "Besides," Bev said, "if that's not her number, we'll just call the Fairview house and ask to talk to her. My brothers and I used to do a lot of prank calling for kicks. I'm pretty good at being believable on the phone. Judy would be proud."

Mary chuckled, rolling her eyes. "When do you think would be a decent hour to call her?"

"Well, first I think we need to get the rest of the Fifties Chix here. No excuses. And I don't care if it's early."

"Thanks, Bev," Mary said gratefully.

"Some day for a picnic," said Maxine, watching the rain slide down the window panes in Bev's kitchen.

Judy was still trying not to giggle at the sight of Mary in one of Bev's brother's old T-shirts. It was better than the soaked and wrinkled PJs Mary had shown up in, Judy was told. Judy would have had a hard time not bursting out joyfully about anything at this point, though; she was on cloud nine after her audition. It was an added bonus that now she was standing in Bob's house.

They were just waiting for Ann to arrive before Mary caught them up on yesterday's meeting with Mr. F and before they tried calling Helga.

"I haven't been here since . . . *you know*," Judy said, glancing around the modern kitchen.

Mary knew: since before the "Travel to Tomorrow" project, when Judy had dumped a chocolate cupcake upside down on Mary's white skirt.

Quiet knocking was barely to be heard from the front of the house. "What is she, a mouse?" Bev sighed, on her way to retrieve Ann.

Bev returned to the kitchen with a glum and nervous-looking Ann. Hugs and greetings went around and they asked Ann why she seemed so agitated.

She whispered. "Is there somewhere we can go that's more . . . private?"

Bev assured them all that her brothers were dead to the world and no one would bother them.

"Even . . . Gary?" Ann asked.

"Everyone needs to stop dating my brothers," Bev said. She was trying to make a joke, but it didn't sound as funny as she'd hoped. She tried her best gentle-caring voice, the one she'd learned from observing her thoughtful friends, and asked Ann what was wrong.

Again, Ann whispered. First she told them about the Holocaust art exhibit Gary had taken her to and then about the painting they'd discovered that she suspected was her grandmother's. They reacted as dramatically as she had, with shock and wonder. She couldn't bring herself to speak the awful words about the fate of her grandmother's paintbrush yet, but she told the girls that she'd made a terrible mistake yesterday telling Gary she'd time traveled.

"Well, James knows and he thinks it's nifty," Mary said, keeping her voice down, too.

"I don't plan on telling Conrad," Bev said.

Judy and Ann looked at Bev with big eyes and Maxine smiled.

"Oh. Yeah. Um, I like Conrad." Bev blushed and her eyes darted around the room, searching for a distraction so she wouldn't have to look her friends in the face. But she needn't have been wary.

"He's dreamy, Bev, really!" Judy raved.

"Good for you," Ann agreed.

"If we keep this up, we'll all be related," joked Maxine.

"Speaking of related," Mary said, "we discovered yesterday that Emily Jackson is Conrad's aunt."

"*Aunt Em* is Emily Jackson?" exclaimed Maxine. "I've heard Conrad talk about her and I probably even met her when I was younger, but I don't remember. What else did you find out?"

Bev let Mary share the details about their meeting with Mr. F. Mary positively glowed when she got to give a report like this. Ironic, considering how much she'd stumbled during their "Travel to Tomorrow" presentation.

She finished by telling them about the note Helga had followed them out to the car to give them.

"What are we waiting for?" Judy squealed. "Let's call her now!"

"I, well, I . . . forgot the note. But Bev thinks she remembers the number," Mary said apologetically.

They gathered around the phone and Ann said, "Why am I so nervous?"

A clap of thunder shook the house and they all jumped and laughed. "OK, let's just call," Maxine urged.

Bev punched in the number. "It's ringing," she whispered. "Who's going to talk—Hello?"

The girls held their breath and Bev fumbled with the phone, passing it to Mary. Mary identified herself politely and asked to speak to Helga. "You said you might have some information for me?"

The girls waited while Mary said, "Yes," and "Oh?" and "Ohh!"

She hung up and paused, which prompted her friends to screech, "Well?!? What did she say?"

"She said she had to clean out Mr. F's office when he retired and he had boxes of papers to shred, but she came across some papers that she thought were interesting and couldn't bear to destroy them. When she heard our names yesterday, she remembered them from the papers—they had our names on them. And the papers are from 1955."

"Our 'Travel to Tomorrow' papers?" shrieked Judy.

"That's what I'm thinking," agreed Mary.

Ann asked, "When can we go see her?"

"As soon as we can get a lift," Bev said.

From the kitchen doorway came Gary's voice. "I'll take you."

10

Hard to Say Goodbye

James couldn't believe that even while Row was upstairs in her room unwell, his parents argued in her living room. Sure, it was in hushed tones, but it was also through clenched teeth. The only reason his dad was there was because he loved Aunt Row as much as James did. Row was James's mom's stepsister, but that didn't matter to his dad.

James couldn't help but replay Aunt Row's collapse over and over again in his head. He knew it was his fault. He'd announced before church the day before that he was moving in with Row. His mom had barely responded that he certainly would not before she'd gotten on the phone to yell at James's dad about it. The next thing James knew, he and his mom were on their way to Row's for a discussion with his dad there.

As his mom was accusing James's dad of pushing James away, Aunt Row—who herself didn't even know that James was hoping to move in with her—dropped to the floor like a sack of potatoes. It was so unnatural, so surreal.

James's dad had exclaimed, "Row!" while his had mom let out a strangled, surprised little, "Oh!"

Hating himself for it now, James had stood rooted to his spot. He wished he had rushed to the other room to get his phone and call for help; but he hadn't been able to take the thought of leaving Aunt Row.

His dad had hollered, "Well, don't just stand there, someone call for help!" and it was James's mom who had scrambled to call 911.

Mrs. F was also called and she showed up at the same time as the paramedics. James was relieved when the paramedics didn't take Row with them, but crushed when a hospice nurse arrived.

Now, nearly 24 hours later, James sat listening to his parents and feeling like he would explode with guilt, cowardice, or both if he stayed in the parlor with them for one second longer.

"I'm going up," he announced, standing.

"Wait until Row invites you up to see her," his mom said.

"If he wants to go up, let him. Just because it wasn't your idea doesn't mean he can't do it," his dad said. While they carefully stoked the kindling for a raging argument, James slipped out.

He tapped lightly on the door and was relieved to hear Row call out nice and clear, "Come in, Jimmy."

"How'd you know it was me?" He entered, closing the door behind him.

"Because your parents aren't that polite," Aunt Row said drily.

James and Mrs. F both nodded knowingly. Aunt Row never spoke poorly of James's parents, but he knew she didn't like the effect their fighting had on either of them. It was one of the many reasons he wanted to move in with her: she didn't pick sides and then tear the other side down. He couldn't live like that any more.

"So, what are we discussing?" James said.

Aunt Row smiled, but James noticed a tear leak out of Mrs. F's left eye under her glasses. He tried not to be alarmed.

"Old friends," Aunt Row said.

"*Forever* friends," Mrs. F said, but her voice cracked.

"What's going on, Aunt Row?" James asked.

Both women were silent for longer than made James comfortable. Finally, Aunt Row said, again in a clear voice, as if she were talking about the weather, that she was not well and hadn't been for a while. When James started to argue that she seemed fine— even as he started to remember strange little happenings with her—she gently said, "I made your parents promise not to tell you. I wanted to myself, so don't be mad at them. Now I'm just saying some goodbyes while it can still be a pleasant prospect."

"It's never a pleasant prospect," Mrs. F corrected sternly. Row put her hand on her friend's and squeezed it.

James marveled that Aunt Row was so calm. Why wasn't she fighting, or doing whatever it took to get better? *Because,* he realized as blood ran cold, *she didn't think she was going to get better.*

"Jimmy, there's so much I want to tell you about this house; it has an amazing history. I'm leaving it to you, you know."

It had been a constant refrain that James had heard before, that he would inherit Aunt Row's house. Someday. But "someday" in James's mind translated to a time so distant in the future it was synonymous with never. Though his happiest memories were in this house, he didn't care about the house; he wanted his aunt. The sleepovers in the guest room that smelled of dust, wood, and maple syrup; Aunt Row teaching him to bake in the kitchen; building frames and arbors for the garden with her—those nooks and spaces in the house were nothing if they weren't filled with Aunt Row.

"This isn't what I imagined it would be at all," said Mrs. F nonsensically.

"So, you imagined it?" Aunt Row ribbed her friend.

Mrs. F disregarded Aunt Row's teasing. "I just thought it would be the three of us again some day. And I thought . . . ." She stopped herself, looked at James, then back to Row. "Well, I just thought this would end differently."

"I thought it might be the three of us again one day, too, honestly. But we all make decisions and we can't change Emily's mind and we can't make those girls do anything. We're all responsible for ourselves and that's it. I learned that long ago."

"It's such a sad way to live," Mrs. F said as a tear rolled down her cheek.

"I'm not sad, May." Aunt Row squeezed Mrs. F's hand again. But James thought she did look sad and he wondered if she'd always looked like that and he had missed noticing it, like so many other things.

"Who do you mean by the three of you?" James asked, his investigative journalist alter ego overriding his manners.

"Our best friend when we were your age—Emily. She ran away after a somewhat traumatic experience and we haven't seen her since," Mrs. F explained.

"And the 'girls'? Who are they?" James knew the answer, not what it meant exactly, but he knew what Mrs. F would say before she said it—

—but she didn't say it. "It doesn't matter. The point is, life will never go according to your plan."

"Nor will death," Row put in.

Mrs. F scowled at her friend. "Stop it!"

"I wish I could."

"What can I do for you, Aunt Row?" James asked, his throat constricted as he held back tears. He wanted to ask her what was ailing her, but if she wanted him to know, she would have said; and she probably knew better than he that he wasn't ready to hear it. She was always protecting him; more than his parents ever had.

"Be happy, Jimmy. Be yourself. What I love about you is that you don't insulate yourself from people. Don't make the mistakes I've made and hold people at arm's length. Being hurt isn't the worst thing in the world." Row's eyes glistened.

When James left the room a few moments later to call Mary, he pondered Row's words. If being hurt wasn't the worst thing in the world, according to Aunt Row, he wondered what was. And then it dawned on him: being alone was.

11

Road Trip

"Am I glad you called!" Mary exclaimed. "Your timing couldn't be better. First, how's Aunt Row?"

James struggled to speak. He hadn't realized that hearing Mary's voice would have that effect on him. "She's . . . not good."

"James! Oh, no. What can I do?"

"That's why I was calling. I think there must something you can do—but I don't know what." James told Mary about Aunt Row's and Mrs. F's conversation about a friend of theirs named Emily and about "those girls *do*ing something."

"Then you need to hear what we just found out," Mary said. "Can we come pick you up?"

She muffled the phone and asked somebody something, and then James heard Gary's voice say, "The more the merrier."

"We'll be there soon," Mary said to James.

James snuck out the back door. His parents were arguing and he didn't much feel like interrupting them and becoming the target of their ire by asking if he could step out for a few moments. They wouldn't miss him anyway.

On the stone patio in the backyard, under the pergola where he was safer from the raindrops, James let his eyes rest on every plant, shrub, tree, and flower of Aunt Row's garden. Everywhere he looked, a memory sprouted and danced before him. He'd learned woodworking from his aunt right over there near the potting shed; she'd showed him to hold a hammer toward the back and not choke up on it—he could use fewer, more powerful blows to drive a nail in. She'd taught him how to paint: the potting shed was four different colors with striped and swirled window boxes. He'd taken her to the emergency room that Christmas when she'd been putting up Christmas lights in the trees and fallen off the ladder. She'd hobbled around on crutches for two weeks and then gotten annoyed and put them away and never limped once after. It was as if she had just decided she couldn't be bothered. All these memories, James wondered, were they dream images of a parallel dimension? What would be his memories had he been in 1955 standing in this yard thinking of his aunt? Would she be up there dying right now if they were in 1955?

Gary's car pulled into the driveway and James was grateful he didn't honk. He dashed through the rain and jumped in the back seat when someone opened the door for him. He was about to wonder how Gary had become involved with all this when he saw Ann in the front. That answered his question. In the back seat, Judy sat on Maxine's lap and Bev and Mary were crammed next to them.

"How's this going to work?" James chuckled.

"You're going to have to double up back there," Gary said.

Mary started to move toward Bev's lap, but James closed the back door and said, "It's OK, Mary."

Blushing, she sat on his lap without objection.

Without editing or omitting anything for Gary's sake—though he had stayed in the car when the five girls had gone in to talk to Helga—Mary told James what Helga had told them and then from the front seat, Ann passed him a small stack of yellowing papers.

"She found these with a bunch of paperwork she was supposed to shred for Mr. F, but she thought they were interesting so she kept them, " Mary said, her eyes ablaze.

The five top pages were titled one after the other, "Travel to Tomorrow, Miss Boggs, May 4, 1955," and featured the five girls' respective names and handwriting. James recognized their unique styles from *The Visible Truth*.

There was a moment of silence in the car as just the *thunk-thunk* of the windshield wipers and the trickle of rain outside played background to James's disbelief as he shuffled through the papers again. "This—are you kidding me? This is insane. This is incredible!" Before he'd felt confident in the fact that his friends had time traveled; but strangely enough, now that he had some sort of proof in his hands, he had a hard time believing it.

"And, you know how you said Mrs. F and Aunt Row mentioned Emily? Well, Helga also gave us this note or diary entry, really, that's a letter to her from Miss Boggs," Mary said. Ann handed James another page.

The car was steaming up and James's legs were already uncomfortable, but he ignored it. *Dear Em*, he read.

"It was never sent," Judy said. "There were a bunch of letters she wrote to her friend that were never sent."

"Because Miss Boggs didn't know where to send them," Maxine added.

"But," Bev said excitedly, "we found Emily! She's Conrad's aunt."

James's mind raced. "Conrad Marshall?" He shook his head, trying to get all the pieces in place. "So where is she?"

"That's the thing," said Mary. "She's in New Orleans. We could just go tell Mrs. F and Aunt Row that we found her, or we could bring her back—"

"What are we waiting for? Let's go get her."

"You have to ask Mom if you can trade cars with her," Bev told Gary.

"Her car is full of cleaning stuff. Besides, she'll never let us drive her car to New Orleans!"

Bev rolled her eyes. "Of course she won't. I doubt any of our parents are going to *let* us drive to New Orleans. But we can't all fit in this car. And we still have to fit Conrad in."

"Uh-huh," Gary said drily.

"We *do*. Emily is *his* aunt . . . she's not going to hop in a car with a bunch of freams from St. Louis!"

Gary sighed. He knew it was true and he knew that he, of all his siblings, had the best shot of using his powers of persuasion to talk his mom into letting them use her SUV. Leaving his friends in the muggy car, he bolted inside to find her. Moments later, he returned beaming. They transferred Mrs. Jenkins's cleaning supplies into Gary's car and then piled in to Mrs. Jenkins's oversized car.

"This is like Diane Dunkelman's car," noted Judy. It was still mind-boggling to see such big vehicles on the road.

"So, where to?" Gary asked and Maxine directed him to her cousin's place.

"You'd better be the one to ask him," Bev said to Maxine. She wasn't exactly sure she was in a position to be asking Conrad to go on a ten-hour road trip.

They waited in the car while Maxine went to talk to him. Bev's heart was beating wildly and it felt like it was clogging her throat. She of course wanted (and they all needed) Conrad to accompany them, but she wasn't sure how the "oh, by the way, we're time travelers" discussion would go down. At least James and Gary would be there. Gary hadn't said much, but the fact that he was going along with them to Louisiana meant he had to have accepted their story to some degree. Or else he was completely head over heels for Ann. (And that would just be pitiful, Bev decided, to not care that there was the possibility he was being lied to as long as he could be with the gal he liked.)

After what felt like an hour, Conrad came back with Maxine. But he didn't climb in the car right away; he proceeded to the passenger side window. Ann rolled down the window.

"I understand you want to contact Aunt Emily," he said. "My mom's flying back to New Orleans tonight. She could give Em a message in person, or we could call her ourselves. I've got her number somewhere."

As Maxine climbed into the back seat, she said, "I tried to explain to him that it's an in-person kind of thing."

While the girls' minds were in overdrive trying to think of how to convince Conrad to go, Gary said simply, "Dude: road trip."

"Sweet. Let me grab my phone and my wallet." Conrad rushed back to his house and the girls burst into laughter.

"Well, that was easy!"

"Seriously, *road trip*," Gary said, and he fist-bumped James, who was sitting in the seat behind him.

Now that the passengers for their voyage were all accounted for, Mary shifted gears. "Now, it's a little over nine hours to New Orleans, and that's if we don't stop for food or gas. Do we want to get food now? When we get there, do we pick up Emily and turn right back around?"

"All I heard were the words *food now*," joked Conrad, so they agreed to stop for snacks on their way out of town and those who had cell phones made calls to parents and loaned the phones to others to do the same. They tried not to snicker when one of them told lies about where they were spending the rest of the day and the night and then "going straight to school" tomorrow.

Judy thought she could probably tell her mom the truth and still be allowed to go, but it wasn't as fun that way, so she told Bitsy she was spending the night with Bev while the others covered their mouths and giggled. Judy didn't like lying—as much as she liked acting—and she told herself she wasn't making up that she would be with Bev. Of course, the rest of the truth— ". . . in New Orleans"—was omitted, making it officially a lie.

Calls done, they turned into a huge parking lot with an equally huge grocery store at one end of it. Upon entering the store, Mary asked, "Do we have a list of some kind?" Everyone laughed.

She reddened. "Well, I just mean . . . ."

"It's OK, Mary. We can come up with a list together and I'll go grocery shopping with you," James said. She thought it was the most romantic thing she'd ever heard.

They split off toward the deli while Gary and Ann headed to the chips and cracker aisle. Bev, Maxine, and Conrad went toward the soda pop and, looking peeved that she wasn't part of a couple, Judy followed them.

When they met up at the checkout at the front of the store, Ann looked at the heaps of food and drinks and said, "How long are we planning on being away?"

"Remember, there are three guys going," said Conrad.

"And me," Bev added.

The girls tried to keep their cool as each one of them ponied up money to cover the $45 bill. Mary mentally listed the things she could have bought in 1955 for $45.

Settling back into the car to start their road trip in earnest, Gary found some 1950s tunes on satellite radio. The girls squealed and sang along, knowing all the lyrics. If there had been any doubt that they were from that era, the doubt was dashed then.

"My phone's ringing!" Judy said. Gary turned the radio down and she answered.

After a brief conversation, Judy hung up and said, "I can't go with you. I got a callback! Can you please turn around?"

Her friends congratulated her, but said they were not making this trip without her.

Ann asked gently, "Is it partly because *he's* not here?"

"Ann!" Judy protested. But her expression revealed that Ann was right.

"Who's *'he'*?" Conrad asked.

"Bob?" Gary guessed, watching for Judy's reaction in the rear-view mirror.

Judy's face flushed.

"What?" Conrad said from the seat behind Judy. "Girl, you are smart and sassy and sweet. Why are you wasting your time on Jenkins? No offense, other Jenkins."

"None taken," said Bev.

"Agreed," said Gary.

Judy said, "But what about my audition? I was a shoo-in for the lead."

"We're all sacrificing things," Maxine said. Then she took a deep breath. "If it makes you feel better, I lost my quill." She detailed her panic upon losing it at the coffee house and all her vain efforts since to retrieve it.

The girls sympathized with her and then Ann confessed that her grandmother's paintbrush had been destroyed by Meshuga, the world's most unruly mutt.

"I didn't know, Ann. I'm sorry," Gary said sincerely.

"While we're on the subject—" Mary started, while Bev burst out, "And I lost my bat!"

"Were these all objects that came with you?" James questioned.

"Came with you from where?" Conrad asked. No one answered.

"Yes!" Mary said to James. "My sewing machine was destroyed. Do you think it means something?"

"Well, it doesn't mean *nothing*," assured James.

"I hope this road trip isn't a mistake," Judy said, shivering slightly.

12

Vagabonds

In the middle of a vision, her mind just went blank. It happened around noon on Memorial Day. The emptiness worried Emily more than the increasingly real waking dreams she had been having. In place of the waking dream, a heaviness settled over Em like a leaden blanket on her soul. For the first time, she wondered if she needed an exorcist.

She told herself to hang on for ten more hours, when Vi would be returning from St. Louis. She wouldn't have to bear the burden alone. Em's plate was full with her ballet studio and when she wasn't mothering her dancers, she was mothering Vi's rowdy kids. Conrad, the oldest, lived in St. Louis with his dad. Probably the most well-behaved of them all and he was mostly out of the picture! A part of Em's daily life were Cassie, as loud, brash, and outspoken as her mama; Ginny, the beautifully talented ballerina; Terrence, obsessed with basketball and convinced if he didn't get into the NBA and make millions his life would be a waste; and twins Micaela and Maiya, who looked nothing alike—Micaela, a bright girl destined to be a marine biologist, took ballet lessons with her Auntie Em; and Maiya was as good a basketball player as Terrence, but nobody told him that. As much as Em loved her family, she adored her studio time for its order and serenity.

Tonight she left thirteen-year-old Cassie in charge of Ginny and the twins—Terrence was shooting hoops with friends—and Em found peaceful refuge in the dance studio at the little desk near the water closet. She had been avoiding a stack of paperwork—or rather, hadn't found a moment of peace and clarity to look it over. There was the dance competition in the fall that she needed to decide on . . . .

She heard crashing sounds outside and jumped up. She tried to remember if she had locked the door. She'd never had break-ins or been mugged before, but it wasn't uncommon in that area. She wondered if it would be cowardly if she locked herself in the tiny bathroom. Her hands searched the stacks of loose papers on her desk. She didn't remember where she'd last seen her cell phone. She despised that thing and often neglected to take it with her. Now she berated herself for not treating it like an appendage of her body like Cassie and Terrence did with their phones.

A floor-to-ceiling wall only five feet wide divided the all-glass front door from the dance studio, giving gawkers restricted access and blocking the wind. The door opened. *Not locked!* Emily said a mild curse word under her breath and leaped into the bathroom, closing the door quietly. She hoped that in a few moments, she'd be laughing about it with whoever was letting him or herself into her studio; but with the black cloud of doom camped out over her lately, she wasn't taking any chances that there had been a harbinger leading to this moment.

"Auntie Em?" she heard a deep male voice call out. It could be a trick. That didn't sound like Terrence, whose voice hadn't changed yet.

She heard voices murmuring and whispering and could barely make out, "Add breaking and entering to running away." "And exceeding the speed limit," someone added.

"Emily Jackson?" The voice was coming closer. It seemed as if a crowd was outside the bathroom door, shuffling toward her. "Auntie Em, it's me, Conrad. You here?"

Conrad? Not an army of ghosts, then. Em turned the doorknob and inched the thin plywood door open. Sure enough, her nephew Conrad, at least six inches taller and more filled out than the last time she'd seen him, stood in the flesh in her studio. With him were two clean-cut white boys and five girls. They were a motley group: the girls wore saddle shoes and circle skirts and looked like they were going to a costume party. One of the girls was African American and reminded Em of someone she once knew, much like the redheaded boy sparked a memory she couldn't place.

One of the girls stepped forward boldly, holding out her hand in introduction. She wore old-fashioned-looking cat-eye glasses and had her auburn hair in a pony tail. "Ms. Jackson, I'm friends with your nephew, Conrad. My name is Mary Donovan and we're here on behalf of Marion Boggs Fairview and Rowena Nolan. We've come a long distance to bring you home."

Em had no idea how she was going to explain to Vi why she was getting into a van—an SUV, one of the girls corrected her —and driving to St. Louis with a bunch of vagabond teenagers. But she knew this: when the girl Mary had said those two names, the dark cloud had dissipated. Just like that: it had lifted off her and disintegrated before her eyes, and the dimensions she'd felt trapped between had merged into a simple, clean one.

Now her house was full: Conrad was introducing his little sisters to his friends, Ann and Gary were pouring sweet tea and distributing it, and Maxine and Mary were in Em's room helping her pack. Em couldn't leave, of course, until Vi returned from the airport—from St. Louis.

"Are either of you dancers?" Em asked. She had so many other questions more pressing than that one, but it was a place to start while she tried to get her bearings and form questions that made sense.

"We're not, but my little sisters are," Mary said. The girl's eyes were roving all over Em's bedroom walls, probably searching for pictures and personal effects. It made Em nervous.

"I know I met you when you were a baby," Em said to Maxine. "But all grown up, you remind me of someone I once knew. But I can't place who."

"Folks say I take after my mama; do you know Gloria Marshall?"

"Well, she must have been at Viola's and TJ's wedding," Em said. "Maybe that's it. Now tell me how y'all came to be the ones to come on down here just for me?"

The girls looked at each other nervously and Mary spoke. "It's kind of a long story. And we have lots of time to explain during the car ride home."

They got the little kids to bed, and it was only a few moments later that Viola returned from her trip, letting herself in the front door in a wave of her usual nervous energy, dragging her bag behind her and muttering to herself about the cost of the taxi. It took her a moment before she noticed the change in her usual surroundings and saw her son coming toward her, his friends sitting in the living room with Em.

"Welcome home, Mama," Conrad said, giving her a hug. From Em's point of view, the hug seemed more an effort to calm Vi before she reacted to Conrad's unexpected appearance than a greeting of affection. It was a tactic she recognized because she employed it frequently herself.

"What in the—?" In her shock at seeing Conrad, Vi seemed unable to give him a full embrace in return and instead put one arm awkwardly around his shoulder.

"He—*they* all—came for me," Em said, approaching Vi for a welcome home hug. "It's a long story—evidently—but there are some friends of mine in St. Louis who want to see me. And this way I don't have to pay airfare." Em flashed the warm smile that she pulled out when she needed to calm Vi.

"Why, that's the strangest—what *friends*? You can't possibly be considerin' going with them, could you?"

"All I can tell you is that this has something to do with those visions I've been having."

"You told them about the visions?" Vi said, alarmed.

"No, this is the first they're hearing it." Em guided Vi to have a seat on the sofa next to James and handed Vi a tall glass of sweet tea.

Maxine came over to give her aunt a squeeze and introductions were made.

"If it's not too personal, would you mind telling us about the visions?" Mary, sitting on the other side of James, said.

Any other day this past month, answering the request would have been overwhelming and out of the question for Em. But she felt clearer—and cleaner, somehow, like she'd taken a brisk shower and come out refreshed—than she had in a long time. Still, she started slowly and chose her words carefully.

"For about a month now, I've been having what we're calling 'waking dreams,' for lack of something better to call 'em. I'll try to describe it to you, bear with me. I feel like I'm overcome with this other place and time like it's playing right over the present. Like having the radio and the TV on at the same time."

"I'm sorry to interrupt," Mary interjected as her friends groaned. "When you say it's been about a month, would you say these incidents starting happening around May fifth?" Her friends seems less annoyed with Mary when they heard the question and they waited on Em's answer with increased interest.

Em and Vi consulted each other with a look and both nodded. "Yes, I'd say that's about right. May fifth, I woke up in the morning—woke right into a vision."

"Do you remember what it was?" Maxine asked.

"Don't go giving away the farm," Vi warned her sister.

"Now, Vi, I don't know what they could possibly do with this information other than think I'm absolutely nuts. I know exactly what the vision was because I've had it several times. I'm in a boat, a large skiff or a row boat; it's the middle of the night, winter, I'd say because it's so cold." Em closed her eyes, summoning the memory. "There are a group of us in the boat. We're desperate, escaping to or from somewhere." Her eyes snapped open. "You," Em pointed at Maxine. "You were there."

Maxine looked stricken. "I . . . I don't think so . . . ."

"She looked just like you, then. There's a baby. Oh! It's the Mississippi! We're crossing the Mississippi; I don't know how I know that, I just do. And in the boat with us—we're all black, except for these two white girls. My best friends."

The room was filled with a silence so full, no one could fit a word in.

Finally, nearly in a whisper, Ann said, "Aunt Row and Miss Boggs."

"What else?" Judy prompted Em. Judy was literally on the edge of her seat about to fall off.

Em closed her eyes and breathed deeply. "We make it! We make it across the river, but two men come with guns—" She stopped herself and her eyes flew open again. "Slaves. We're making our way to freedom. I didn't see that until just now!"

Maxine said slowly and with portent, "Emily, did the woman who looked like me have a quill?"

Without pausing to think, Em remembered, "Yes, because I gave it to her. I stole it and I gave it to her as a gift for being free."

"Was her name Gin?" Maxine asked barely louder than a breath. When Em nodded yes, Maxine said, *"My great-grandmother."*

It was unclear who in the room gasped, but all were spell-bound by the evolution of events as Em revealed them.

Something occurred to Em. "Your great-grandmother? How would that be possible?"

"That's where our story comes in," Bev said.

"Like you said, we have a long drive ahead of us. I don't think we should wait a moment longer," Em stood up.

Viola didn't even consider objecting when her sister climbed in the car.

"Oh! Vi! My classes! Can you—"

"Consider it done. Don't worry about a thing. Just call me and keep me posted." Vi's usual zeal was replaced by a calm warmth. She gave her son a hug and a kiss and said goodbye to her sister.

And they were off.

13

Grounded

On the way to New Orleans, there had been plenty of opportunity for singing, car games, and a few red-light-green-lights. Judy had even begged for Gary to let her drive a shift; but only Gary, Conrad, and James had their drivers' license and her "offer" was duly declined.

The journey back from New Orleans had a decidedly different tone. Radio off, sailing down the interstate in the dark, there was no thought of stopping for gas or bathroom breaks just for the fun of it. Instead, Emily told them about the visions she'd been having and Mary, Judy, Maxine, Bev, and Ann took turns telling Em about how their lives had changed since the morning of May fifth.

Soon it was Mary's turn, and she relayed all the most current information about Twig and Reggie. Then she gave Em the letters that Helga had salvaged, and as Em read them, her tears started to flow. She reached into her bag and brought out the typed letter that she had memorized because she'd read it so often and wondered at its meaning.

"I'm so sorry to do this, but I think your taking me back to St. Louis might be a mistake. I should have told you about this sooner, but I have a letter, too—from Marion and Rowena— and they requested that I never come back to St. Louis."

As Mary reached out to look at the letter, it was snatched away from her suddenly. It took Mary a moment to realize that Em wasn't pulling the letter away, the car was careening out of control.

"Is everybody OK?" James said from the front seat.

The car had jerked to the right, to the left, and back to the right before spinning halfway and skidding sideways to a hard stop before it had the chance to slide down an embankment. After the road noise and the screeching, the SUV sounded eerily quiet—except for the windshield wipers that James had accidentally bumped into the "high" position when he'd tried to right the car.

"I said, is everybody—"

One by one, they answered James, checking themselves and whoever had been sitting near them. They appeared unscathed, but none of them could quite catch their breath. With liquified knees, they climbed out of the SUV. It seemed like fresh air was in order.

"Are you kidding me?" James called from the back of the car, kicking a tire.

The crowd moved to the back and saw what James was cursing: two blown out rear tires.

"What do we do?" asked Judy, who was clearly shaken up. She was shivering, even though it was ninety degrees out at three in the morning.

Mary held up her cell phone. "Call for help."

"That's a no-go," Gary said, holding up his phone. "No reception."

Those who had phones pulled them out and held them in the air, turning in funny circles searching for a signal.

A semi rushed past them, kicking up dust.

"A trucker wouldn't have done *that* in the '50s," sighed Ann.

Another truck, this one with "FairVan Lines" painted on the side, blew bast not a moment later. "Let's flag down the next one," Mary said.

Agreeing unanimously that it was their only option, they lined up on the side of the road and started waving widely as soon as the next pair of headlights bore down on them. The truck slowed, changed lanes, and flew past.

"Do they think we're playing a game?" wailed Judy.

Em's aunt-ing skills kicked in and she wrapped her arm around Judy. "It's OK, the right one will stop," she appeased.

And the next one did stop.

The trucker pulled about 50 yards ahead before coming to a stop on the shoulder.

"Need a tow?" he called out as he walked back toward them.

"Actually, we need to use your radio. We can't get a cell signal and my daddy's Reginald Fairview," said Mary, who had noticed the FairVan Lines logo on the side of the trailer. FairVan Lines was one of Mr. F's subsidiaries. Her friends glared at her. What was she up to?

"Come on, then, I'll see if I can git through to dispatch for ya," the driver said, waving Mary toward him.

"What are you *doing*?" Maxine whispered, pulling Mary back.

"Look, we don't just need a tow; we need to get back to St. Louis as quickly as possible. We can't call our parents—even if we wanted to. And let's face it, another adult might not be such a bad idea, and one who has the means to get us back is even better."

The guys, Maxine, and Bev shook their heads no, but no one offered any better ideas, so Mary followed the trucker to his cab and James skipped to catch up to her.

"I'm so sorry, Mary. I slammed on the brakes to avoid hitting an animal and I just lost control."

"It's OK, James. Everyone's all right. We'll figure this out."

"I shouldn't have come; I shouldn't be away from Aunt Row this long and now I've made it longer." He slipped his hand in hers and they walked the rest of the way to the driver's truck door. Mary didn't know if she could possibly take any more emotions: from the news about Aunt Row, to finding Emily Jackson, to getting shaken up in the car, and to now holding James's hand, she was about to either crumble into dust or explode into a million crystal shards. Either one would be no less surreal than walking down the interstate in Mississippi in the middle of the night holding James O'Grady's hand.

The trucker helped Mary and James into his cab and pulled out his two-way radio. Identifying himself, he told dispatch he needed to make a person-to-person to Reginald Fairview. The dispatcher, a woman, snorted.

"Like that's gonna happen, Earl."

"I got his daughter and her friends here on I-55 in Mississippi in a broke-down car. You want I tell him you said I should leave 'em?"

She sighed. "You owe me, Earl."

"Nah, Fairview owes *me*," he muttered.

They waited a few moments and Mary wished the dispatcher had left the line open so they could hear the call to Mr. F. Earl tried to make polite conversation, but both Mary and James were brief with their answers, as they didn't want to miss being back in touch with dispatch.

Finally, she crackled back on. "Took some doing, but I got a hold of Fairview. Got the man out of a dead sleep. Says he don't have no daughter."

Mary grasped the radio out of Earl's hand and pressed the talk button as she'd seen him do. "Tell him it's Mary Donovan and I'm with my friends and Emily Jackson and we're bringing her to St. Louis."

"Did you catch that?" the dispatcher said. Mary didn't know who she was talking to until she heard Mr. F.

"I heard. Next time call my office and leave a message," he said gruffly and hung up.

"There's your answer, y'all."

"Thanks, Francine. Over and out," Earl said.

Earl replaced his radio and Mary's heart sank. She knew it was wrong to lie—she was already caught in a big one just by having taken this road trip—but she'd hoped Mr. F would have some pity on them and at least try to help. But it was not to be.

"Our cell phones aren't getting a signal," James said. "Would you mind calling a towing service for us?"

"No, sir, I don't mind. What else can ya do?"

Earl called dispatch back again and Francine said, "I already seen where you're at on my GPS. Someone's comin', but it could be at least an hour."

Mary couldn't contain herself. "An hour!" She might soon have to give up the idea that she'd make it home in time for school. And she'd certainly have to admit that she was not going to get away with the sneakiness and lies that had caused this debacle. There was nothing to do but prepare to be grounded for the rest of her life.

She and James returned to the group and reported their destiny: wait over an hour for a tow.

Their previous conversations were put on hold; Em climbed into the front seat to rest and Gary lay across the rear seat for a nap. A few of them did jumping jacks to stay awake and the rest of them chatted quietly about nothing of significance.

After about an hour, James pointed north toward the horizon. "That looks like a UFO . . . what *is* that thing?"

Those who were't napping followed James's gaze. They became more and more intrigued as the light headed right for them, accompanied by a loud motorized chopping sound.

"That's not a UFO, that's a helicopter!" Conrad said.

Gary woke up and everyone who was inside the SUV hopped out. They couldn't believe it when the chopper landed in the field next to them about 100 yards away.

A gentleman hopped out and and started walking toward them.

"That's Mr. F!" exclaimed Mary.

When he reached them, he yelled over the engine and the blades, "Someone here call for a lift?"

14

Together Again

Reginald Fairview explained that he hadn't known there would be quite so many people needing rescuing and that his helicopter only held six. The Fifties Chix and their new friend Emily were the natural choice for a ride in to St. Louis and the guys agreed to wait for the tow, hoping to either have the car repaired quickly or find a way to get home by late morning.

Goodbyes were hard; they'd started this adventure together and didn't want to take next steps divided up. As the girls walked toward the sleek silver chopper that looked like a robotic insect, Gary yelled, "Anna, I believe you!" and blew Ann a kiss.

They settled in to the helicopter and were given earphones with mics to communicate with each other. As they lifted off, Mary remembered her fear of heights. Having never flown before and never even been in a skyscraper, her stomach lurched and she was sure her face turned green. Emily, who was sitting next to her, looked equally uncomfortable and held Mary's hand.

Though a confined space, the inside of the helicopter was luxuriously appointed with tan leather bench seats and glossy wood trim. The wide windows opened up to gently rolling hills, rows of trees, and lit-up towns in the distance. As they rose higher, Mary dared a glance to see if she could find the Mississippi River out the west-facing window. On one side of the cabin, a wet bar and mini refrigerator stood waiting to be of service. Mary couldn't conceive of having a snack or even being able to hold her hand steady enough to drink a bottle of water.

To distract herself, Mary struck up a conversation with Mr. F. "Why did you decide to come for us?" Mary learned she didn't have to yell because the mic system amplified her voice loud and clear in the headphones. If things hadn't felt futuristic before, they were officially in the future now!

"If you called for me and said you were my daughter, I thought you must really be in trouble."

"We didn't exactly tell our parents we were leaving town," Maxine said.

"I suspected that." He smiled. "I also suspected that your taking this trip has something to do with my wife."

"Mr. F, meet Emily Jackson," Mary introduced them. "One of your wife's best friends."

Mr. F gave Emily a long look, much like the Fifties Chix had when they'd confirmed that Emily was decades younger than Mrs. F and Aunt Row. But instead of denying that he knew of her like he had the other day, he leaned across the chopper and put his hand out. "Nice to meet you at long last."

"So you *have* heard Mrs. F talk about Emily?" Mary asked, not completing the rest of her thought: *even though you told us the other day you have never heard of her?*

"I have," he admitted.

"Mr. Fairview," Emily started. "Can you give me a little warning? Will your wife and Rowena be terribly unhappy to see me?"

When Mr. F said he didn't see why they would, Emily once again drew the letter out that she carried with her. She handed it to Mr. F, who told Em to call him Reggie.

He read the note with interest and Mary swore his eyes watered. She had yet to see the letter herself and was curious why Mr. F found it so moving. She got her answer soon enough.

"This is from 1955?" he asked Em.

She nodded. "I suppose so. I found it among my things about a month ago. I—well, it's a long story, but I have reason to believe it is authentic and meant for me."

"It is meant for you. But I wrote it, not Marion." Mr. F was pained.

Now Mary had to ask to see it. She read it quickly and gave it to her friends to read, too. The letter was signed *Marion Boggs Fairview* and essentially told Emily to stay away for good.

"I'm afraid I don't understand," Em said.

"It was a terrible decision on my part, made hastily and made out of fear. And yes, it was written in 1955. To you."

Mary wondered why Mr. F was so readily confessing his hurtful deed and realized it must be because within a few hours Em would be reunited with Row and Mrs. F and the truth would be out. Her heart filled with a sadness that felt like a toxic liquid. *James would never do that*, she told herself, and the ache eased a little—at least for herself. She was tempted to give Mr. F a piece of her mind, but she could tell by his expression that her words would be redundant.

"I'm terribly sorry, Emily. It wasn't supposed to be like this."

Mary glanced at her friends. There was so much she wanted to say to them and share with them and she could see that it was mutual. It appeared they were at long last getting to the bottom of it all, but when they did, Mary hoped they wouldn't hit with a painful thud.

As dawn was breaking, the Fifties Chix and Emily, escorted by Mr. F, pulled in to Aunt Row's driveway. With a pang of guilt, Mary noted James's car. She'd been so tired, it hadn't crossed her mind to call on him and check where the boys were. James, Conrad, and Gary were who knew where with Mrs. Jenkins's disabled car. And she knew where James wanted to be: at Aunt Row's.

The house seemed gloomy. Even the sky was a steely purple and didn't have the glow of promise so often present at this early time of day.

Em, still nervous to see May and Row even though Mr. F had taken full responsibility for writing the letter, asked the others to go inside first. They filed in, Em the last one, and were surprised to find Mrs. F in the parlor downstairs. Next to a dim lamp, she was nestled in a light blanket on the wingback chair, reading a book.

"Girls!" She jumped up. ". . . and *Reggie?*"

The Fifties Chix hugged her and Mary and Judy started crying.

"We brought someone to see you," Ann said, urging Em forward.

Mrs. F opened her mouth to speak, but no words came out. Then she pushed through the girls and fell on Emily, wrapping her in a hug.

"It's me, Em—" Emily started.

"I know."

"I'm so sorry—"

"I know. It doesn't matter. Can you come up with me to see Row?"

"Of course!" Em's eyes glistened, crystal clear. No visions, no memories; it was all here, now, real, only this time she wasn't just telling herself that; it was true.

They clung to each other for one more long moment and then May took Em's hand. She kissed her husband on the cheek as she passed by him to go upstairs to Row's room. Mr. F's cheeks reddened, perhaps his guilty conscience coloring his countenance. A long, difficult conversation was in their near future.

The Fifties Chix collapsed on Row's living room furniture, realizing how exhausted they were. Mary stood back up.

"I'll see what Aunt Row has in the kitchen. Can I get anyone something to eat or drink?"

"Have a seat, Mary; I'll get donuts and bagels and coffee." Mr. F headed for the front door, but then paused and turned around. "You know how you told the dispatcher at FairVan Lines that I was your dad? I hope it doesn't sound strange, but you all do feel like my daughters now." He smiled and went out for breakfast.

Several moments were spent in silence, breathing, thinking, not thinking.

"Should we wait here? Or go up? Or go home?" Judy whispered at last.

"I'm not ready to go home," Maxine said, and everyone agreed.

"I think we just wait here then," Bev said.

"What do you think it's like? After all these years?" Mary said, gesturing to the second story where the reunion was taking place.

"Probably like no time at all has gone by," said Ann.

"For all we know, it hasn't. Now what year is it?" Maxine joked. It felt good to chuckle.

"If getting them back together was the only reason we—" Mary lowered her voice out of habit "—*time traveled*, then it's all been worth it."

"Agreed," the others chimed at once.

And just when they felt at peace and happiness began to well up in them, Mrs. F appeared. Quietly, she said, "Rowena is gone."

15

Cold Comfort

Every minute seemed to last a year and by fifth period, Maxine felt as though she'd aged one hundred times over. She had been convinced—all the Fifties Chix had—that finding Em and reuniting her with her two best friends had been a victory. They'd never imagined it would have such a sad ending. Even though Em and Mrs. F had both assured the girls that morning that they were grateful the three of them got to be together to say goodbye, Maxine thought it was an incredibly cruel twist of fate and a question played and replayed inside her like a steady drumbeat: why? Why? *Why?*

"Uh-oh, look who's here. Hope Mary can control her temper," Judy leaned over to whisper to Maxine when Skip, the sub, entered the classroom to cover for Mrs F.

Maxine was grateful for the start of a smile Judy's comment gave her. Even Mary, who'd overheard, showed a glimmer of amusement.

The boys had returned at lunchtime from being stranded with Mrs. Jenkins's SUV in Mississippi, and not without consequences. Gary had had to notify Mrs. Jenkins about her car's whereabouts and it came out that Bev had been with him. Mrs. Jenkins promptly contacted Mrs. B about Ann and it had been a domino effect from there. James was devastated that he'd not been able to say goodbye to Aunt Row.

So now, compounding mourning the loss of Aunt Row, was the prospect of slugging through school only to go home to outraged parents. Maxine swung between resignation and hopelessness, the resignation a dull ache and the hopelessness an acute pang. Rivaling the two for her deepest resentment, though, was the powerlessness. They had been hoping to outwit life, and now it seemed they had no chance of outwitting death.

"You are not to participate in any tribute to that woman," roared Gloria Marshall at her youngest daughter.

"You don't understand," Maxine said feebly. She despised that phrase, so often uttered by teenagers. Usually, it meant that a parent was out of touch with youth, but in this case, neither her mama or her dad could possibly understand that Maxine had time traveled and was lost in her own life, and that Mrs. F had the key.

"You're right, I don't understand. I don't understand how a teacher could put you in a position over and over again that compromises your integrity. First, she encourages you to write that article—"

"She had nothing to do with—"

"—Second, you defend her to that *Diane Dunkleberg* girl—" despite her mom's serious tone, Maxine had to stifle a laugh that threatened to bubble up "—and get in trouble for that and third, she asks you to take a road trip in the middle of the night and lie to your parents about it."

"She didn't ask us to take the road trip," Maxine insisted. "Daddy. . . ."

"I'm with your mama on this, baby. Don't 'Daddy' me. You said you took the road trip for her. Why couldn't you call Emily and give her Mrs. F's number?" *Uh-oh.* If her dad was firmly in her mom's camp, Maxine had lost her case for sure.

"Needless to say, you're grounded. Only coming to and from school, no calls to friends, and absolutely no participating in a tribute to *that woman.*"

Hearing her mama address Mrs. F as *that woman* in such a bitter tone constricted Maxine's heart and she found it hard to breathe. She raced to her room, resisting the urge to slam her door, and threw herself on her bed, reaching for her—

Then she remembered the quill was gone.

"What do you mean, you 'missed the callback'?" Bitsy White cried. "After all that work Roger did with you?"

Judy didn't have the energy to point out to her mom that for once—actually, in most cases—this had nothing to do with Roger Streeter. Roger was the last person to be affected by the fiasco that Judy was enduring. But neither was he to blame; and

Judy had just learned that taking her frustration out on an "inno-cent" bystander wouldn't help assuage her despair. So she resigned herself to listening to her mom's rant.

"I will just call the school and talk to the director—or go up higher if I need to—and get you in for that callback."

Judy was horrified. That would be worse than missing the callback for a legitimate reason.

"It's not the school's fault or the director's fault. I missed it myself," Judy argued. She eyeballed the cats, who were basking luxuriously in the sun streaming in the kitchen windows. After yesterday's cloud-clogged skies—was that only yesterday? Judy marveled—Desi and Dragnet were taking full advantage of the rays today. Judy did not appreciate the cheerful blue skies on such a tragic day.

"Well, just because you made a mistake—"

"Can't you just be a normal mom?" Judy stood up from the kitchen table. "Can't you just be mad that I sneaked off with my friends to drive to New Orleans and lied to you about it?"

"Well, I am upset about that. But the school needs to under-stand that everyone makes mistakes—"

"Then let me make them! Be a mom and let me be a kid."

Bitsy threw her hands up, exasperated. "Well, then, fine. You're grounded. Is that what you want?"

"It's a start," said Judy.

16

One of the Family

Mary rushed in the door apologizing.

"Why, Mary? What happened?" Nana said.

"I'm sorry I lied to you."

Nana was folding laundry and Mary's mom, Jane, was on the phone, but she quickly got off. "About what?" Jane asked.

Mary realized too late that word hadn't gotten back to them about her whereabouts the night before. She had texted her mom that she'd be spending the night with Judy (which of course, she was). She faltered. There was still a way out of this. And besides, they'd shown how little they cared when her diary and sewing machine had been destroyed.

"I didn't spend the night with Judy last night; or rather, I did, but not at her house. We went on a road trip, and it's a long story, but we were trying to do something nice for Mrs. Fairview's retirement by bringing back her long-lost best friend, but when we returned this morning, her other best friend passed away and it's been a horrible day and I can understand if you want to punish me. I don't blame you. But I am sorry." Mary took a breath and her grandmother and mother stared at her, incredulous.

"Where did you go?" her mother asked.

Mary wanted desperately to name a destination closer to home, but she was on a roll with being honest. "New Orleans."

Nana gasped. "Mary! I'm stunned! What would make you lie to us like that?"

"I think I know." Mary's mom spoke in a gentler tone than usual. "Were you feeling unheard because of the incidents with your sewing machine and diary?"

"I was, but that's not the real reason I went and didn't tell you. I didn't tell you because I knew I really needed to do this and I don't think I can explain to you why."

Mary's mom approached Mary and embraced her, stroking her hair like she'd used to do when Mary was little. "I'm sorry that yesterday we didn't handle what happened to your stuff very well. And I'm so thankful you were honest with us just now, and that you're back in one piece."

"Does that mean I'm not in trouble?" For the first time all day, Mary glimpsed a faint ray of promise.

Nana and her mom laughed heartily. "Oh, sweetheart. You are in a great deal of trouble. But we still love you."

Bev sat in Gary's room and sympathized with him. It was much better than sulking by herself in her own room. Every time she'd seen Bob that day, he'd given her dirty looks. She understood why. Since she was tiny, Bob had almost been like a twin; they'd done everything together and they'd been partners in crime. He felt left out that Bev had sneaked off with Gary instead of him. She wanted to explain that he'd done it to himself by not participating in the *Visible Truth* project for Maxine. He'd essentially chosen pleasing Diane Dunkelman over his sister and his other friends, and now he'd missed out on an adventure. And . . . on being in hot water with their parents.

And Bev wasn't sure what kind of an adventure today was. It was more like torture. And hearing her mom rant at her about how Bev had disappointed her and how Bev had always been counted on to be the "good one" in a household of boys made Bev realize that her place in the family was defined by the other family members and their maleness. Not that Bev denied that she had broken the rules. But she'd gladly pay the price for breaking rules like lying; she just didn't think she should be punished for not being the girl her mom had hoped for.

"I wonder how much trouble Ann is in. Do you think her mom will let us Skype?" Commiserating with Gary was growing tiresome.

Bev didn't know what Skyping was or if Ann's mom would let her do it.

"You understand this isn't all about Ann, right?" Bev grumbled. "Mrs. F lost her best friend and—"

"And you time traveled. I know. I do want to help, but I don't know what we can do."

"Well, with all the reading you do, you must read about time travel. Are we missing something?" Bev spun around in Gary's swiveling office chair in front of his desk. He lounged on the bed with his laptop computer. Speaking of missing something, he'd missed his deadline for his paper; he was still working on it, but with a much different attitude than when he'd started it.

"When people time travel to the past, it's usually because they're charged with changing something to improve the future. When someone travels to the future, well . . ." Gary thought about it. "I would think it would be to take some kind of information back to present day."

Bev stopped twirling and thought about that. "What information could we possibly bring back to 1955?"

Gary shook his head. "Yeah. So weird that your 'present day' is 1955. How nice for you to be able to time travel right out of being grounded."

"Do people ever stay? Do they time travel or hop dimensions and then just stay?" Bev wondered. Then she sighed. "I miss Conrad." It felt good to say that openly and it brought her a sense of comfort.

"I miss Ann."

Oh, brother.

"I can't believe it's really you," Ann said, happily perplexed.

"You are as lovely as I could ever imagine."

Ann stared into the screen. Why had she been so reluctant to have a video call with her cousin before? She had wasted so much time not taking advantage of things like this—technology, friends, family—since time traveling. Irina was a living, breathing person on the other end of the "line," on the other side of the world. Ann had of course seen pictures, but hearing

Irina and seeing her facial expressions—especially those that Ann recognized as similar to her own—was magical.

After both of her parents had yelled at her—and it took a lot to get her tatty that fired up—and she'd received a phone call from the curator confirming that the artist who'd painted *Family of Man* was named Nikka Brajer, Ann had needed to talk to somebody and she knew it had to be Irina.

"I think we could be sisters, yes?" Irina laughed. Ann was flattered. She appreciated the ease and natural beauty her cousin exuded. Her short, dark brown hair fell in half-curled locks around Irina's face, framing her soulful brown eyes.

Ann complimented Irina on her English; she loved listening to Irina because it reminded her of her mom's 1955 accent. Irina asked after the family and then asked about Gary. Still digesting their whirlwind trip to the South and back and the consequences, Ann skipped over it to tell Irina about the trip she and Gary had made to the Holocaust art exhibit.

"And you think this artist is related to our family?" Irina asked with big eyes.

It was hard to have a conversation because all Ann wanted to do was watch her cousin and marvel that she was having a real-time conversation with her.

"I'm pretty sure," Ann said. She didn't feel comfortable mentioning the paintbrush that had been their grandmother's that Meshuga had wrecked.

"How long will the exhibition be in place? Perhaps I can see it in person!"

"Oh, really, Irina?"

"Yes. I believe I've talked Father into letting me come to the States to meet you and to get out of Belgrade this summer. What do you think?"

"I think it's the best news I've had in a long time."

17

This is Your Life

Mary flipped through the pages of her diary with a heavy heart. She saw entries from 1955 and from after waking up in "present day," all scribbled over, some portions beyond recognition. She put aside—or tried to—her astonishment that her siblings would deface something so precious of hers, and she read whatever entries she could, looking for some clue or hint of what to do next.

Barricaded in her room with her disabled sewing machine and a half-finished quilt, Mary looked from the diary to the window and back again. They'd had some reprieve from the rain, mocked by blue, sunny skies when they'd all felt so low, and now the rain and wind had kicked up again. Nana had warned Mary after dinner that there was a tornado watch and if she heard the siren for a tornado warning to come quickly to the basement. She wouldn't be able to finish the quilt in time for Mrs. F's "This is your Life" tribute, but what was the point? Mrs. F probably wasn't coming back to school anyway and there would be no completed square from Aunt Row—or Emily—and they were who really mattered.

Mary felt she'd let her teacher down in a multitude of ways. Whatever reason they'd time traveled for, Mary was still missing it. Everything—like the limp pile of half-sewn quilt squares—was unfinished. Mary did not do well with unfinished.

On top of that, her heart broke for James, who was grieving his aunt. Mary's phone had been confiscated, so she couldn't even talk to him and offer him words of comfort.

She almost confused the knocking at the door for the wind blowing against the house.

"Mary?" her mom called as she opened the door a crack. "Your teacher called your phone and I answered it; I thought it might be important. You can talk to her, if you like. But make it quick and no other calls."

Mary jumped up and gratefully received the phone from her mom, mouthing *Thank you* before shutting the door.

"Oh, Mrs. F, how are you?" Mary wished she could climb through the phone and hug her.

"I'm doing well, Mary, thank you for asking. Of course, I miss Row terribly, but the three of us were reunited, thanks to you. I'm calling because I realized that I've not been helpful to you and the other girls. I'm trying to remedy my mistakes; Row's teaching me that. So I have something for you and, well, I know it's getting late, but would you and the girls be able to pay me a visit tonight? I'm staying in the garage apartment at Row's."

A crack of thunder sent a shiver down Mary's spine. "I don't know how we can possibly come see you. Unfortunately, we're all in a bit of trouble because of our trip to New Orleans."

"Oh." Recognition dawned in Mrs. F's voice. "Oh, I see. You didn't tell your parents where you were going. I understand that; my mother never would have let me do that at your age."

"Let me see what I can do," Mary said. After what her teacher had endured losing her friend and discovering she'd been betrayed by her husband, if Mrs. F was asking for something, Mary wanted to come through.

Mary sneaked to the door of her room to see if she had enough privacy, but didn't sense her mom was waiting outside the door. She hurriedly called Judy first. They hatched a plan to sneak out of their houses and meet at Aunt Row's. Mary would call Ann, and Judy would call Maxine and Bev.

An hour later, Mary tiptoed down the stairs and out the front door while her mother and Nana were distracted and the kids were curled up on the sofa. They had refused to even try to sleep in their own beds with the frightening weather. When Mary latched the front door quietly behind her, she found she was once again ill-prepared to be running around in a downpour. No raincoat and no galoshes.

A few blocks from Aunt Row's, Mary felt a welcome sensation: adrenaline. She might be grounded the rest of her life, or worse, but she was going to see Mrs. F and find a way to help. A rumble of thunder that seemed to come up from the bowels of the earth and not from the sky, shook Mary to the bone. But she didn't care.

The tornado siren that sounded minutes later, however, was a cause for concern.

"Mary!" Mrs. F yelled over the siren and the howling winds. The trees in Row's yard were bent sideways and she wondered how they didn't snap off. She stood at the back door, steadying herself as the wind attempted to whip her around, waving Mary over to the storm cellar. From the back of Row's house, Mrs. F could see the girls arrive one by one except for Maxine and Bev, who'd arrived together. Mary was the last to arrive and Mrs. F rushed over to her to direct her to safety.

Once inside, Mrs. F slammed the door closed and locked it as she'd seen Row do once when there was a tornado warning during a sleepover. "I tried to call and cancel when the siren went off, but the power was out. I was hoping none of you would come; but here each of you is after all. We'll make this quick."

"It looks exactly the same," said Em, who was staying with Mrs. F, looking around the tidy cellar. The girls hugged each other and huddled together, gas lamps set up around the place flickering and adding to the ominous mood.

"Guess she never did get it electrified," Mrs. F said. "Well, this isn't exactly what I had in mind, but what else is new?"

The girls laughed nervously.

"I should have done this weeks ago, but it's not like there are any hard and fast rules. You get a sense of how it all works only by following your heart."

Something clattered across the cellar doors and the girls jumped. "It's OK, we're safe in here," Mrs. F guaranteed. She'd been assuring them they were safe since the start of all this, but she had nothing to go on except faith; and now her faith—and theirs, she was sure—was wearing thin. "First, I have a confession to make to Emily."

Attention turned to Em, who sat between Maxine and Ann, holding their hands.

Mrs. F held out her arm and pulled back her sleeve. "I didn't lose the watch. I mean, I did, but—"

"I know, May. I read your letters."

"How—?"

"The girls found them. I guess Reggie had kept some."

"Actually," Mary piped up, "it was Helga. She was supposed to shred the letters, but she kept them and gave them to me and I gave them to Emily."

"I always knew I liked Helga. I'm terribly sorry for lying to you about having the watch, Em." Em accepted her friend's apology with a gentle nod. Mrs. F slipped the watch off her wrist and the girls held their collective breath. "Like I said, I should have done this weeks ago. Mary?"

Mary stood up, smoothed her wet skirt, and stepped forward.

"This is for you. It's for all of you, but I'm entrusting it to Mary." Mrs. F grasped Mary's left hand and tenderly, decorously slid the watch onto her wrist and fastened it. Mary's face registered her surprise. She looked back at her friends and they seemed equally shocked, but no one spoke up to say the watch shouldn't be on her wrist.

"What do we do with it?" Mary said dumbly.

"You can go 'home' if you want to. It takes getting used to; you have to concentrate and fill your heart—your mind, your whole being—with love. That's about as specific or scientific I can get with you."

"What if we don't want to go home?" Judy asked.

Em nodded in understanding and Mrs. F said with a warm smile, "Well, that is a choice you can make; just ask yourselves, is what you *want* secondary to what serves the greater good?"

Outside, the storm began to quiet as quickly as it had kicked up. The other four girls, now standing, had gathered around Mary to inspect the watch and touch it. "Are there any questions I can answer for you?" Mrs. F asked her protégés.

"So many questions," Maxine said.

"Where do we start?" Ann said. "I mean, with the questions. But I guess, where do we start with the watch?"

"With the watch, start by working together. I learned that lesson the hard way," Mrs. F said.

"I have a question," Mary said. "Do we have to go home or can we go anywhere—any*when*?"

"I suppose it can be any 'when,' but again, I recommend working together."

"We will," promised Judy and the others agreed.

"Won't you miss the watch?" Ann asked their teacher.

"I'm sure I will; but I've had enough adventures thanks to that watch to last five lifetimes. It's your turn now . . . this is your life."

18

Back in Time

The world had been washed clean. Half the moon was in shadow, but the half that shone sparkled on the slick dark surfaces of new baby leaves, tree trunks that looked dunked in ink, and sidewalks and streets that were scrubbed clean as if in anticipation of a photo shoot.

The girls had said their goodbyes to Em and Mrs. F, uncertain about the next time they would see them. As they left Aunt Row's together and before they broke apart to go their separate ways, they met at the corner of the fence in the front yard, drenched in moonlight and feeling washed clean themselves.

Mary couldn't stop touching the watch on her wrist, feeling the surprising weight of it. When Mrs. F had first placed it on her, it had felt cold and clunky, but now it was warm against her skin, and even soft, as if it were velvet instead of metal.

"Let's see it again," Judy said, and Mary held it up in a shaft of moon beam. The watch glittered.

"Well, when to first?" Mary laughed, not really joking. Besides the physical weight of the watch, she felt the power that came with it.

"We should go overnight tonight," Ann said. "I'm scared to, but let's face it, we're going to be in a lot of trouble with our parents in the morning." The others snickered, but mostly from nerves. They knew Ann was right about going and about their parents.

Maxine sighed. "I can't believe I'm recommending this, but I think we need to go to—"

"1945," the other four Fifties Chix said in unison.

"Exactly," confirmed Maxine. "For Mrs. F, and for Em."

"And for Aunt Row," Mary added.

"Well, we're in agreement, which is what Mrs. F wanted," Bev said. "So now what? How do we do it?"

"We're all—" Mary glanced at Judy and amended, "—most of us are believers, so I imagine it's like praying. Just focus on 1945, on Em and Row and Mrs. F, go deeper and bigger than ourselves and . . . *trust*."

"That's beautiful, Mary," Ann breathed.

"So, this is it," Bev said. She'd never looked so vulnerable and uncertain. Her eyes even filled with tears.

"It'll be OK," Maxine said. They gathered for a group hug.

They decided to go to their separate homes and be in their rooms, where they'd traveled the first time. "See you in the morning," they said with shaky confidence, avoiding saying the word "goodbye."

Mary's alarm clock rang and it sounded like it had been amplified five times over. It was a good thing she'd set it the night before; she'd gone to bed very late after getting dressed down by her mother and Nana when the tornado siren had gone off and they'd realized she was gone. She'd stuffed her bed with pillows, which when they'd been discovered, had at least tipped off her family that she'd deliberately left instead of being kidnapped. But that hadn't helped Mary's case much since she had already been grounded.

So when the alarm sounded, calling Mary out from a dead, dreamless sleep, she was surprised and dismayed. She had concentrated so hard before falling asleep . . . . But it hadn't worked. She woke up in her room, everything the same.

Danny ran by her door, screaming and pounding it as he went by. Yep, everything was definitely the same. Mary considered pulling out her diary to write down her thoughts and get mentally prepared for the day, but the thought of seeing it in its defaced condition was too depressing. She might be grounded but at least she had one last day of school to see her friends. And James.

She opened the bedroom door as Maggie dashed by.

"Hey, where's your SpongeBob t-shirt?" Mary said.

"What's a spongebob?" Maggie asked, giving her a weird look.

Mary proceeded to the bathroom, wiping her glasses on her nightgown as she went. But when she pushed the door open, she froze. Her heart stopped, her blood slowed, her eyes dilated. *Old bathroom.*

"Nana!" she cried, running downstairs.

Old living room, old TV, old kitchen. Nana in the kitchen fixing bacon. Mary couldn't help it; she threw her arms around Nana.

Nana laughed. "Well, good morning, sleepyhead. Good thing you didn't sleep through your alarm on your big day."

"The last day of school?" Mary asked, trying to figure out when the watch had sent her. *Wait, where was the watch?*

"No, silly. Your big social studies assignment, the 'Travel to Tomorrow' project."

"That's *today*?" Mary almost yelled.

Nana laughed. "You *were* sleepy. Now go sit down and eat your breakfast so you can get your energy up."

Judy never woke up early, but she'd set her alarm for it this morning. She hadn't told her friends, but the director of *110 in the Shade* had said she could make up her callback audition before school started. She'd also told her mom she was going to see Mrs. F and her friends last night. Probably everyone else had sneaked out, but her mom had offered to drive her. Judy had declined. Having her mom drop her off at the curb would have spoiled the caper.

This morning, she was tempted to text Bob. She'd been in pretty regular touch with him and yesterday afternoon he'd told her that he and Diane had broken up for good!

She glanced around for her cell phone and realized she must have left it in the kitchen. She brushed her hair one hundred times and found a pair of pedal-pushers that looked more con-temporary than her usual poodle skirt.

She was still grounded, but her mom told her she could go to rehearsals for the musical if she got the part. Judy had a feeling she could probably do just about anything she wanted during her probation if she asked. But they were on shaky ground, so Judy definitely planned to ask instead of assume.

Since it was early, her mom hadn't yet come to wake her up to ask if she wanted a latte, so Judy figured she'd make coffee herself. But as she walked into the living room, she did a double take: white furniture, lemon yellow walls . . . 1950s Hollywood.

Judy's heart raced and she sat in the nearest plastic molded chair, but stood up again. She paced. *It worked, it worked, it worked! No*, she thought. *This isn't 1945.* Had she not concentrated hard enough? What if her friends were in 1945 and she was—here, or now, whenever she was. She instantly yearned for her cell phone, which would tell her what date and year it was. She had an idea and quickly made coffee for her mom.

After forever percolating, enough coffee was ready to fill a cup and she took it and tapped on her mom's bedroom door.

"Good morning," Judy said cheerily.

Bitsy roused herself. She wore her light blue, lace-trimmed sleeping cap to cover her rollers. Judy felt nostalgia tug at her heart when she saw her in the cap. "You're up early, Jujube. And you've already made coffee! Thank you. What day is it?"

I was hoping you could tell me. "It's a good day."

"I know, silly. I was teasing. It's your 'Travel to Tomorrow' report day at school."

A lump formed in Judy's throat. "May . . . fourth, then?" No chance for a lead in the school play.

"Yes, and I have a presentation to help Roger get prepared for."

"You know, Mom, you do as much work as—if not more than —Mr. Streeter. Maybe you should be his boss."

Bitsy laughed. "Wouldn't that be something!" But she paused, and Judy could tell she might give that a little more thought.

After hugging her mom and giving Desi and Dragnet extra snuggles, Judy brushed the cat hair off and headed for school, afraid of what she might discover.

Maxine rolled over, stretching deeply. She hadn't gotten nearly enough sleep to feel rested, but neither had she stirred or had strange dreams. She was surprised the other bed hadn't been slept in and wondered where Mel had ended up last night. Then she sat bolt upright: the quill. It rested on her desk, next to her bed.

She flung the covers off and leaped to grab the quill—gently, of course. She nearly wept with relief. Who had found it and placed it there? Then last night came into sharper focus. Her prayer before falling asleep: she'd focused on Row, Emily, and Miss Boggs—she'd pictured Miss Boggs, not the older Mrs. F. She thought of her friends, and found herself making a thank you list, hoping with all her heart that she and her friends, as well as Row, Emily, and Miss Boggs, could have friendships that lasted a lifetime. Something occurred to Maxine then and she bolted out of her room, down the hallway, and into the kitchen.

Where the framed picture of the President had been, now the red apple cookie jar sat. Her mama's slick white cabinets were back hanging on the clean white walls. Her daddy walked into the kitchen in his blue jumpsuit with "John" embroidered on it.

"Daddy!" Maxine rushed to her father, flinging her arms around him and nearly knocking him over. She wanted to tell him something, but decided against it. Then she changed her mind again. She whispered, "Never let them call you 'boy.'"

She waited for him to chuckle, or play it off lightly, but he didn't. He held her tight. "I'll try, Max."

"For me. And for Melba. I don't care if you get fired. It's worth it."

He gave her a long final squeeze. "Love you, girl."

"Love you, too."

For the first time, Ann realized what it had taken for her mother to run two households, the Jenkins' and her own—and that one entirely consistent with the highest kosher standards. She leaned against the kitchen counter that morning, marveling, with Meshuga sitting innocently at her feet (Ann's paintbrush was miraculously untouched in her room). The place was immaculate. Both parents were already at work, Ann's first clue that she was in another "when." She'd nearly wept when she'd seen the brush intact on her dresser with her other painting supplies.

Now standing in the kitchen, she was ashamed that it had taken so much for her to see the sacrifices her parents had made; it had taken cheering and supporting her friends, seeing Row die, and falling in love with Gary.

Wait. Was she in love with Gary Jenkins? A smile spread across her face in acknowledgment, but then quickly faded. She had no right to be happy right now and she wasn't "here" to frolic with Gary (besides, she couldn't assume he felt the same way about her. It was another time and they didn't know each other. Yet).

Alex came in and greeted her sweetly, his normal little self, *yarmulke* in place on his head. "Are you having breakfast? Can you make me a bagel, please?" he asked.

Ann studied him quietly without moving or responding. Then she said, "Alex, did you know that Franco Dunkelman is a punk?"

Alex shrugged. "Yeah, I guess so. But he's my best friend."

"Just don't ever let him talk you into doing something that goes against who you are, promise?"

"I promise. Can I have lox, too?"

19

Friends Forever

"Hiya, James!" Mary said, standing at her locker surrounded by her friends. James gave a shy smile and a little wave and kept walking.

"Go easy on him," advised Ann. "We'd better go easy on everybody."

"Someone still has to explain this to me," said Judy, on the verge of a whine. "I thought we were going to go to 1945."

"Can we *please* keep it to a dull roar?" pleaded Bev, concerned as ever about being overheard.

Mary was distracted by James's response and had to drag herself back to the conversation with her friends. She had been downright giddy when she'd gotten to school, but she quickly realized the need to focus.

"I don't know about you, but I mostly prayed to help Mrs. F —I mean, Miss Boggs—Emily, and Aunt Row. So maybe going to 1945 wasn't the best way to do that," Maxine said. "We must have traveled to when we could be most helpful."

"Well, I am glad we get to do our report over," Mary said. Her friends burst into laughter. "What?"

"All this, and you're happy to do schoolwork!" They couldn't stop howling.

Mary was about to protest when she saw it, too. She did love her assignments. She giggled along with them until the bell rang.

"Do we practice at lunch?" she said as her friends were about to disperse.

"I think we'll be fine winging it at this point," Bev said.

"More importantly, I believe," Ann said, "is our meeting at the five and dime later today when we see Miss Boggs."

Bev had lost her appetite. While she was grateful to be with Judy and Ann at lunch, her heart and mind where elsewhere: on her morning waking up again in 1955. And on Conrad Marshall.

She had been thrilled—but confused—to see her bat next to her bed upon opening her eyes. She, like Judy, wondered why they weren't in 1945. With caution, she had ventured out of her room to see her 1955 house, pre-remodel, and had smelled eggs and toast. Though she had known what to expect when she came into the kitchen, she'd still caught her breath at the sight of her mother and Mrs. B.

Mrs. B had had her kerchief on her head, which Bev now knew had religious significance—she wondered if her mom knew that—and her mom had already been in full makeup, with perfectly coiffed hair and a pressed apron over her dress and crinoline. Bev had shuddered involuntarily when she'd caught a glimpse of the pointed, high-heeled pumps that her mother tee-tered on.

"Good morning, darling," Mrs. Jenkins had said, pouring Bev a glass of orange juice.

This was not a world where she could go to the diner with Conrad Marshall for a burger and a game of pinball. Bev had felt a sob catch in her throat and she swallowed it, pushing it down.

"Good morning, Mom and Mrs. B." Presuming this hadn't been a dream, Bev had felt bad that Ann would be waking up with no mother to make her breakfast. Bev had given her mom a kiss on the cheek and taken her orange juice to the kitchen table. So long ago, she and the girls had sat at this table to plan their "Travel to Tomorrow" presentation, and look at them now.

As Bev had forced down her breakfast, not entirely hungry but knowing that she would need the energy, she'd paid close attention to how her mom and Mrs. B worked together. She'd never noticed it before. They barely had to speak, their heads bowed together, one passing something off to the other; it reminded her of an old couple who'd been together so long they finished each other's sentences. Or a team.

"You know what would be cool? You two should start a busi-ness," Bev had said. "You work so well together and you keep this house running. Think if you provided services like that to other families."

Mrs. Jenkins had tittered, "You silly goose. Always teasing."

"I'm not teasing. I guess what I mean is, thank you for all you both do. I hope you know you've really inspired me to reach for excellence and follow my heart. So, um, yeah. Thank you."

Bev had brought her dishes to the sink and her mother had stared in her at awe. Bev hadn't realized until that point her mother had never seen her voluntarily do anything remotely domestic. "Maybe if we all help you two out, you can have a little more time to look into it." Bev had smiled.

She'd left the kitchen to get ready for school, Mrs. B and her mom gaping after her, astonished.

And now sitting at lunch, she couldn't help but think of how her mom and Mrs. B were trapped in this era. She doubted they had the wherewithal to break out of their expected roles to do something new.

"Bev?" Ann said gently.

Bev shook her head and came back to her friends at the lunch table. "Sorry," she mumbled.

"Are you thinking about *C.M.*?" Judy whispered.

Bev couldn't help but chuckle. She appreciated Judy's discretion, but she found it sad, too. From now on, unless they went back to the future, her whole life would be about discretion, secret codes, and sneaking around. Assuming Conrad found her at all appealing in 1955.

"I am thinking about Conrad," Bev admitted, looking across the cafeteria at him. "And our moms, Ann. I hope they're happy."

"I know, Bev. But one thing at a time. Let's do what we can for Miss Boggs first."

"Do you really think she'll come again?" whispered Judy.

They sat at their marble table at the five-and-dime. The whole place seemed smaller and more cramped than they remembered. Bev had to adjust to the disapproving glances they got from other patrons because four white girls were sitting with an African American girl. Seeing Maxine take it quietly with such dignity made Bev want to scream.

"I know she'll come," Mary declared.

"Do you think she knows what's happened? With us going back and forth, I mean? She looked so flabbergasted by our presentations today."

"I still think my favorite part was when Maxine said in 55 years we'll have an African American president!" grinned Ann.

"Well, I know we improved our grade this time around," Mary said, taking a noisy sip of her cherry phosphate and then giggling.

"Fifty-five percent!" hooted Bev, Maxine, Ann, and Judy.

"Look! Miss Boggs, over here!" Judy waved at their teacher as she walked in the door.

Miss Boggs's eyes lit up and she made her way to their table. She pulled her gloves off as she approached and Mary choked upon seeing her wrist. The watch.

Miss Boggs stood over their table and her lily-of-the-valley perfume wafted around her like a delicate cloud. "How do you think we did?" Judy asked, echoing herself in another dimension.

"Well, I still have to grade your papers tonight, but overall I was pleasantly surprised. How do you think it went?"

The girls all nodded enthusiastically and smiled. "It was a lot of fun," Ann said, oversimplifying the facts.

"I was surprised how much we learned," Bev put in.

"You know what the main thing we learned is?" Mary said. "That we'll be friends in fifty-five years. Don't you think so, girls?"

"Absolutely!"

"Definitely!"

"I know so."

"Certainly," they all agreed, and Miss Boggs flushed in a most satisfying way.

"That's wonderful to hear," she beamed.

"Oh, Miss Boggs," Maxine said. "I noticed that you went to school with my aunt—well, Conrad's aunt—Emily Jackson? I was looking through some old yearbooks and saw you with her. Did you know she's living in New Orleans? You probably knew that. Anyway, she found out that she has a sister; that's Conrad's mom. A lot of people, including her for a long time, thought she was an only child."

Miss Boggs's smile froze and she looked like she was going to pass out. Bev, closest to her, jumped out of her own seat and helped Miss Boggs sit down.

"Are you OK?" the girls asked. Judy fanned her with a napkin, wanting to do something to help.

"Can we please get some water?" Mary called to the soda jerk. The girls were all standing now, gathered around Miss Boggs.

"I really am fine; I'm so sorry. In fact, I'm better than fine. Maxine, how did you—? I actually *didn't* know where Emily was and have very much wanted to know." She scrutinized Maxine, and slowly took a look at each of the girls surrounding her. "How did you . . . ?"

"I guess the assignment just got us thinking about friendship and time, and all that stuff," Judy said. "It probably sounds goofy, but I'm learning to appreciate a message my dad wrote me before he was killed in combat. He said 'love always.' I think he meant love always makes room."

"What a splendid message, Judy," glowed Miss Boggs.

"Yeah, and I learned from my mom that following your heart doesn't always mean going after a guy," Bev said. The others nodded, appreciating Bev's subtlety. How else could they warn her about Reggie without spooking her?

The kid from the fountain set down a glass of ice water and Miss Boggs gratefully took a sip.

"I'm learning to speak up. We all may not have the same color skin, but we all have a voice," Maxine said, and Miss Boggs nodded, eyes twinkling with tears.

"What about you, Ann?" Miss Boggs asked.

"Oh, I'm learning that sacred things aren't limited to holidays or temples or rites. The sacred is in everything and it's my privilege as an artist to look for and reproduce grace wherever I see it."

"That's lovely, Ann," said Mary. "I think that goes just swell with what we learned from our 'Travel to Tomorrow' project."

"Remind me what that is, again?" Miss Boggs said.

"Friends are forever," they answered in unison. And then they laughed at how tacky it sounded . . . but they knew for sure it was true.

20

"Never Ask for Tomorrow"

"I found her!" May burst in the back door and into the kitchen.

The new Mrs. Nolan jumped and put her hand over her heart. It had been going on a dozen years that she'd been married to Row's dad, but May still referred to her in her own thinking as the new Mrs. Nolan. No one could take the original Mrs. Nolan's place.

"I'm so sorry," May said, realizing that her exuberance was interrupting a solemn moment. Row was sitting with the new Mrs. Nolan, whose daughter, Grace, had come by for a visit. Grace had a son named James O'Grady who was a student of May's. Row adored him and referred to him as Jimmy. After having him in her classes, May could see why James was so adored by his aunt. He was bright, intelligent, and thoughtful.

May noticed that Grace was dabbing at her eyes with a lace hanky. "I can come back," May offered.

New Mrs. Nolan said, "It's all right. We're just finishing up here. My little Gracie is getting a—" she whispered the next word conspiratorially "—divorce."

Grace let out a wail and May offered her condolences.

After the two of them left May and Row alone, Row said, "I can speak from experience, she is hard to live with; but no one deserves what she's going through."

"My heart goes out to James," added May. "He'll need his friends and his Aunt Row right now."

Row agreed and expressed her willingness to do whatever she could for James as she retrieved a clean glass for May and filled it with lemonade.

"As I was saying . . . I found her."

"Who?"

"One guess."

"Don't toy with me, May." Row said. She knew who her friend was referencing and they'd been looking for years with many false leads.

"I'm not kidding you. I found Emily. She's in New Orleans with her sister."

"She has a sister? How happy she must be! How do you know this?" Row asked.

"I just came back from seeing my students at the five-and-dime. One of them, Maxine Marshall, told me she was looking through old yearbooks and saw us with Em and recognized her —as her cousin's aunt—and thought I might be interested to know."

Row paused. "Hm. Interesting. Don't you find that a bit—"

"Peculiar? Absolutely. But Row, we've found her. It's what we've wanted. Can we borrow your dad's car to drive to New Orleans? We can go as soon as I get out of school tomorrow."

"My bags are packed. What about you?" Row asked. "Don't you have a date with Reggie this weekend?"

"I'm calling to cancel right after we're done here."

Row took the kerchief, which she was wearing for her garden work, out of her hair and shook her blond hair. "What if she doesn't want to see us, May? She's left us to worry all these years; she knows where we live and she hasn't reached out."

"We have to at least try, Row. I don't want to live a lifetime not knowing, do you? Besides, what do we always say about friends?"

"Friends are forever." Row smiled, touching the gold heart pendant around her neck. "You're right, of course. Count me in."

Row pulled her dad's 1954 black Crestline to the base of the apartment stairs and laid on the horn. She was trying to be funny because she knew May was just as eager as she to get on the road and find Em. May did see the humor, because she came out of her apartment, giggling, one large suitcase and a cosmetics case in tow.

"And just how long do you think we'll be gone?" hooted Row.

May struggled down the wooden stairs, continuing to laugh. A warm breeze had kicked up and it was a glorious day for a ride. May wished Row's dad's car was a convertible like Reggie's.

She'd wrapped a scarf around her head and wore her dark glasses anyway. The windows would be down for sure.

As Row helped May load the suitcase into the back, Row joked, "You never bring this much when we 'travel.'"

"I'm not used to traveling this way!"

Row drove the car through downtown St. Louis to hop on I-55 South. They decided they'd take two days to New Orleans, finding a motel in Memphis overnight. "Maybe we'll see Elvis," said May, feeling downright giddy.

"Don't let Reggie hear you talking like that," Row warned in jest.

As they sped down the interstate, May noticed how much had changed between Row and her just since they'd had real hope of being reunited with Emily. May had been writing Em letters that she didn't know where to send and she brought them along. She knew it was silly, but she wanted to prove to Em that they had never given up on her. It reminded May of something she wanted to talk to Row about.

May turned the radio down and said, "Row, I've been writing Em letters and I decided to bring them along. Now, don't make fun. That's not why I'm telling you. Some of the letters are missing and I think Reggie may have them."

"Why would Reggie have them?"

"I think he may have *taken* them." May paused. "They're letters that mention . . . our *time travels*. His family has so many businesses; it might sound paranoid, but what if he's interested in me . . . well, for time travel as a business venture?"

"Oh, May. Well, there's a conversation you need to have with Reggie then."

May put her hand out the car window and felt the warm wind rush against her fingers. She made her fingers into a spear shape and cut through the distance to New Orleans and then spread her hand again, pretending she was slowing the car by pushing against the wind. "What if he rejects me when I tell him the truth?"

"Goodness, May, I would think *he* should be worried *you* might reject him for violating your privacy!" Row exclaimed.

Well, that, too, May thought. She knew she needed to make some hard choices between time traveling and settling down with Reggie anyway. And now it seemed the choice had been made for her: when she'd woken up that morning, the watch had been gone, nowhere to be found. Many other mornings she had time traveled and woken up without it, only for it to turn up later. But this time it was different. She hadn't remembered time traveling. She *had* tried to use the watch the other night to make her five students time travel—

"Row," May said slowly. "How is it that a day after those girls did the presentation I assigned, we're about to find Emily?"

Row took her eyes off the road long enough to glance at May. "You would know better than I would, wouldn't you?"

May nodded and smiled, but she wondered.

The next day, any doubts May and Row had had as they'd driven down the street to Emily's ballet school in the Ninth Ward of New Orleans were dissipated when Em recognized them coming through her door.

Row had said simply, "You can run, but you can't hide." And Em had burst into tears and flung herself at her friends while a class of small ballerinas looked on uncomfortably.

"I've been working up the nerve to send you a letter to see if you'd forgive me for running away without a word! How did you find me?"

May told her it had been through Em's nephew and his cousin, who were students of May's.

"Oh, you're a teacher, Marion! How marvelous!" Em couldn't stop hugging her friends.

"Emily?" Row said, pointing to the students. Em laughed and asked if Row and May could stay for class and they could talk afterwards.

"Since we drove down from St. Louis to find you, I think we can wait half an hour to talk to you," agreed Row.

After class, Em took Row and May to meet her sister Viola and Vi's young children. Long after Vi and the kids had retired to bed, May, Em, and Row talked, giggled and cried together. Em confessed why she'd run away after their journey to the Civil War. Seeing firsthand how slaves had been treated, finding out she was part African American, and then discovering how her white grandparents had been ashamed enough to give away a sister Em never knew she had just because they'd been worried her sister was "too dark"—it had all been too much. Em had wondered if she was even the girl her friends thought she was and she admitted she had been afraid that the more they knew about her, the bigger the likelihood they would reject her.

"Why, Em, it sounds as though you don't know us at all," May cried.

"I know; that's why I stayed away so long. It all sounds so foolish now. I did find Viola, though, and her adopted parents took me in so readily. It was nice to have a family, but I missed my friends. I hope we can make a fresh start."

"We never gave up on you," Row said. "May even wrote you letters every week!" She paused. "And about that fresh start . . . I'd like to make one, too. It's exhausting holding everyone at bay."

"By 'everyone,' I assume you mean Tommy Twigler?" May was only half teasing.

"That's not who I meant!" Row insisted, but her cheeks reddened. May and Em barely stifled their giggles and it felt like old times. Or . . . new times.

By morning, Em knew she wanted to move back to St. Louis.

It was just sitting there, on top of her sewing machine, as if someone had walked in while she slept and arranged it there. The gold watching caught a single ray of morning light and winked at her. Mary was mystified and fortified at the sight of it. The last time it had been on her wrist was when Mrs. F had given it to her and Mary had then woken up in 1955 without it; now, on May 5, 1955, the day that she had not yet a chance to live, the watch was in her possession. This had to be a sign—a good one.

She gingerly lifted it and inspected it once again, this time in the light of a new day. She turned it every which way and noticed it was engraved on the back: *Liebe kann nicht nach der Zeit enthalten sein. Die Liebe ist ewig.* Oh, how Mary suddenly wished she spoke German! Dare she ask Miss Boggs to translate?

After appreciating all the watch's beautiful details, with great ceremony, she placed it on her wrist, once again feeling the weight of its importance and power. She took a few moments to admire how it looked on her, noticing the second hand whirring so fast it was almost invisible; and then the practical side of Mary kicked in. She was a fifteen-year-old girl; what would she be doing wearing such a watch to school? As equally careless would be trying to find a hiding place for it in her bedroom. After all, her diary and sewing machine hadn't fared well.

She searched for a creative solution and came up with an idea. It might not be the best one, but it was the only one she had: she pulled on her favorite white angora sweater. She'd have to find another solution as they headed into warmer weather, but for today, she could keep the watch close and covered.

She pulled out her diary to discover that not only was it undamaged, but the last diary entry was dated May 4, 1955. Mary laughed, but she felt a pang, too. No record of her adventures in another dimension, except for the lessons learned that were written in her heart.

Patience wasn't Bev's strong suit. It had been more than 24 hours since she'd woken up in 1955, and she'd had no contact with Conrad other than seeing him in fifth period. Now, having made it partway through her second day, she was getting antsy. She'd have to accompany Bob to baseball practice after school and find a reason to talk to Conrad. It was very forward of her, and where she hoped it could lead—to hanging out with him off the field—was risky for both of them.

So when he came into the classroom right as the bell was ringing and went past his desk to get to his, she held her breath. She smiled at him and he winked back. Winked. Like he knew, he remembered! Bev's heart raced. Was it possible? She did not concentrate on one single thing Miss Boggs said, even though she had been looking forward to having her young teacher back at the head of the class and she was telling them what she thought of their "Travel to Tomorrow" presentations.

Then she stepped aside and let the next group give their presentation, and the suppressed giggles of Bev's friends moved Bev to pay closer attention.

Indeed, their predictions were about as silly as the ones the Fifties Chix had initially made: robots, pills for breakfast to replace all daily meals, flying cars, and the fall of communism only when America bombed the Russians to smithereens. Bev began to appreciate the Fifties Chix' original presentation, however, because at least they had addressed things like civil rights, women's rights, the arts, culture, and family life. Their talk yesterday, of course, inspired by firsthand experience, had been leagues away from even their best initial guesses.

After school, Bev told her friends that she was going to baseball practice with Bob. Judy, of course, enthusiastically encouraged it and volunteered to escort her. The others saw Bev's real intention of picking up where she left off with Conrad.

"Just be careful," Ann cautioned.

"I thought you approved of Conrad and me," Bev said.

"She does, and we all do," Mary assured. "But we all need to tread lightly. We're starting from scratch and we just have to take it one day at a time. And we don't know how safe it is for *him* to be seen with you."

"It's just not fair," Bev said, giving her foot a little stomp.

The four other girls guffawed; first, because it was so unlike Bev, and second, because it was such an understatement.

"Hey, Maxine," Conrad said from a few feet away. He was too shy to approach the group of white girls standing with his cousin, and Bev was relieved he probably hadn't heard anything. "I have practice today, but if you're hanging around, I can walk you home after. I'm having dinner at your place tonight."

"That would be swell," Maxine replied. "Actually, we're all going to watch practice, aren't we? You know Bev, don't you? Her brother Bob plays."

Bev could have kicked herself for blushing, but she was unprepared for this turn of events.

"Yeah, sure I know her. Hey," Conrad said.

"Hiya," Bev said, barely above a whisper.

When he left, Bev gave Maxine a playful punch.

"You're welcome," Maxine laughed. "Now seriously: be patient."

Patience wasn't Bev's strong suit. It had been more than 24 hours since she'd woken up in 1955, and she'd had no contact with Conrad other than seeing him in fifth period. Now, having made it partway through her second day, she was getting antsy. She'd have to accompany Bob to baseball practice after school and find a reason to talk to Conrad. It was very forward of her, and where she hoped it could lead—to hanging out with him off the field—was risky for both of them.

So when he came into the classroom right as the bell was ringing and went past his desk to get to his, she held her breath. She smiled at him and he winked back. Winked. Like he knew, he remembered! Bev's heart raced. Was it possible? She did not concentrate on one single thing Miss Boggs said, even though she had been looking forward to having her young teacher back at the head of the class and she was telling them what she thought of their "Travel to Tomorrow" presentations.

Then she stepped aside and let the next group give their presentation, and the suppressed giggles of Bev's friends moved Bev to pay closer attention.

Indeed, their predictions were about as silly as the ones the Fifties Chix had initially made: robots, pills for breakfast to replace all daily meals, flying cars, and the fall of communism only when America bombed the Russians to smithereens. Bev began to appreciate the Fifties Chix' original presentation, however, because at least they had addressed things like civil rights, women's rights, the arts, culture, and family life. Their talk yesterday, of course, inspired by firsthand experience, had been leagues away from even their best initial guesses.

After school, Bev told her friends that she was going to baseball practice with Bob. Judy, of course, enthusiastically encouraged it and volunteered to escort her. The others saw Bev's real intention of picking up where she left off with Conrad.

"Just be careful," Ann cautioned.

"I thought you approved of Conrad and me," Bev said.

"She does, and we all do," Mary assured. "But we all need to tread lightly. We're starting from scratch and we just have to take it one day at a time. And we don't know how safe it is for *him* to be seen with you."

"It's just not fair," Bev said, giving her foot a little stomp.

The four other girls guffawed; first, because it was so unlike Bev, and second, because it was such an understatement.

"Hey, Maxine," Conrad said from a few feet away. He was too shy to approach the group of white girls standing with his cousin, and Bev was relieved he probably hadn't heard anything. "I have practice today, but if you're hanging around, I can walk you home after. I'm having dinner at your place tonight."

"That would be swell," Maxine replied. "Actually, we're all going to watch practice, aren't we? You know Bev, don't you? Her brother Bob plays."

Bev could have kicked herself for blushing, but she was unprepared for this turn of events.

"Yeah, sure I know her. Hey," Conrad said.

"Hiya," Bev said, barely above a whisper.

When he left, Bev gave Maxine a playful punch.

"You're welcome," Maxine laughed. "Now seriously: be patient."

Mary made dinner for her family: her famous meatloaf, mashed potatoes, beet salad, and green bean casserole. When her mom was looking relaxed toward the end of the meal, Mary took action.

"Mother, I have a kooky question for you. I hope you'll bear with me," she started.

Her mother urged her to continue while Nana looked at her, skeptical. Perhaps she heard the curious tone in Mary's voice, or maybe she didn't think the deed of accepting Mary's delicious family dinner would go unpunished.

"I've been thinking about my dad a lot. And I'm just wondering if we might be able to contact him so I can see him every once in a while. It might be nice for the children, too."

Patty stopped playing with her mashed potatoes long enough to stare at Mary and then looked to their mom for her reaction.

Mary's mother carefully placed her fork on her plate and put her elbows on the table, folding her hands above her plate, first like a church and steeple, then fingers flat. Mary couldn't tell if she was angry or just considering.

Jane cleared her throat. "I've actually been communicating with your father and he has requested to see you. I just didn't —"

Nana touched her daughter's shoulder. "It'll be all right, Janie."

"I wanted to protect you children, but it may be in your best interest to have a man in your life. So if you are requesting it, I will let him know that you have some interest in possibly seeing him."

"Oh, Mom!" Mary stood up to hug her mother and her apron string trailed in the beans on her plate. She didn't care. "Thank you. Thank you for being such a good mom *and* dad to us. You, too, Nana."

Mary was pleased at the progress, but as she took a bite of beet salad, she thought of James. His parents' divorce was just at the beginning. She wondered how he was faring.

That night, Mary discovered the beautiful blue fabric that she'd used to make her dress, the one James had liked so much, sitting in a neatly folded pile with her sewing notions. The dress, like her damaged diary, had gone back to—or remained in?—its original 1955 form. Mary was all too delighted to sew the dress again, and much as she had been in reliving the month of May, this time in 1955, she was more attentive to the details that mattered and less careful about the things that didn't.

For example, knowing how much James loved that dress, as Mary sewed it, she didn't give one thought to impressing him. Instead, she thought of how she could be a good friend to him during the trying time with his parents. So at the sock hop on Saturday night, when he approached her and commented on her dress, she didn't think to blush or argue or get tongue-tied. She gratefully accepted the compliment and asked who his favorite poet was.

He seemed taken aback, but smiled. "I don't mind Lord Byron, I suppose. Gosh, I don't know if anyone's ever asked me that before," he said.

"Well, now they have," she smiled back.

"And your favorite poet?"

"'Love is anterior to life/Posterior to death,/Initial of creation, and/The exponent of breath.' That's Emily Dickinson. I 'don't mind' her," Mary said, borrowing James's words.

The music continued to blare all around them—not ideal for a meaningful conversation, but Mary didn't care; she'd missed talking to James. *Rock Around the Clock* came on. "Oh, I adore this song!" Mary raved.

"Let's dance!" James held out his hand and they did. It was the first of many.

"You are not going to believe this!"

"Try us," Bev said.

"*The Rainmaker*! This summer, our school is putting on *The Rainmaker*! And auditions are on Monday!" Judy was flushed with excitement.

It was a Saturday afternoon on Memorial Day weekend. Mary, Maxine, Bev, and Ann had been sitting on Mary's patio fanning themselves and enjoying overly sweet lemonade when Judy had raced around the house and through the back gate, waving a flyer announcing the auditions.

Mary, covered head to toe—including a straw hat that extended out a foot around her head—to protect her from the sun, put down her embroidery to congratulate Judy.

"That *is* swell," Bev said, marking the place in the book she was reading about the history of the All-American Girls Professional Baseball League. She'd rather be throwing a baseball than reading about it, but she wanted to know how she could start her own women's team, so research was the order of the day.

"You don't understand," Judy insisted. She confiscated the iodine and baby oil from Ann to slather on her bare arms, careful not to get any on her pale lavender sundress. "Remember—before—I was called back when I auditioned for *110 in the Shade*? Well, this is the play that that musical was based on. I love the universe."

The girls laughed. Judy's new, oft-repeated expression was "I love the universe." She used it whenever there were connections to their time traveling exploits or when things fell into place. Or when Bob noticed her.

"How's the diet?" Ann asked. She didn't open her eyes, just continued to lay in the bright sun and see the colors dance through her eyelids. She said she was wanting to do a series of paintings "from the inside out," and was doing research on light. She was also snoozing on and off. She and the rest of the Chix had taken on the task of holding Judy accountable for her new "diet."

"It's fine, I promise. I eat everything my mom makes for me and I haven't weighed myself since you told me to stop. Also, I only look in the mirror to make sure I don't have broccoli in my teeth."

"Good girl," Maxine encouraged.

Just days after arriving in 1955, the four others had confronted Judy. They'd noticed she hadn't been eating and was making comments about her weight. They had known that simply telling Judy that in fact her body was just fine the way it was wouldn't be enough, so they told her all the things that she did that they loved, and how needed she was—and none of it because of how she looked. Maxine had been especially helpful in talking about how frustrating it was to be judged on looks and that it was a trap she didn't want to see Judy fall into by judging herself that way. Then they had told her that she was required to eat at least three normal meals a day, starting with the meatloaf Mary had made. And they all said she was forbidden to drink coffee, especially as a meal.

"What about—?"

"Bob?" Bev had said. "If Bob doesn't have the good sense to see you for who you really are, he's not worth ruining your life for. You have bigger fish to fry than Bob Jenkins."

Back on the patio in the sun, Mary took up her embroidery again. "I just know you'll get the part, Judy; and we'll all be there in the front row, cheering you on."

Maxine's new favorite quote that she wrote in her diary with her beloved, recently recovered quill was, "Write in recollection and amazement for yourself," by Jack Kerouac. While her friends seemed to welcome their return to 1955 with their new knowledge, Maxine was filled with dread. How white people viewed people of her skin color hadn't changed; at least not yet. What had changed was her friends' passivity. They had now became outspoken advocates for her and for civil rights, and if ever she felt she should remain quiet about something, they spoke up so she didn't have to. "Not to silence you," Ann had explained, "to strengthen you."

When the time came at the end of May for her to turn in to James her essay called "Useless Generation," James approached her with an "idea" he and Mary had come up with called *The Visible Truth*, a newsletter filled with potentially radical content about civil rights. Maxine wrote an essay to contribute called "Hopeful Generation," a less combative title than the one she'd written originally.

21

Till the End of Time

May, 2010

"A wedding! I wouldn't miss it!" Maxine crowed. She couldn't stop smiling.

A moment later, she called her assistant, Jacob, into her office. "Please send flowers to my friend Judy White; she's getting married! You have her address in "contacts" on the shared network on the computer. And make sure the flowers are bright, colorful, and exotic. None of this plain yellow mums business."

"Isn't Judy your friend that vowed to stay single forever?" Jacob asked.

"That's the one," Maxine laughed. "And let me know when the Senator calls back. Even if I'm on the other line, I want to talk to her about the bill."

"Of course."

Maxine was grateful to have found such an efficient administrative assistant. She would be sorry to lose him; soon he'd move up to paralegal and then she imagined he'd apply to be an associate in her firm. He would be a good addition, but for now she was just happy that his hard work meant she could get out of the office at a decent time.

She turned in her chair and gazed out at the view. Washington, DC was never lovelier than when the cherry trees shimmered in blossoms, but the lush green leaves of mid-spring were a close second. For years, Ann had promised to come do a painting from Maxine's office window of the trees in bloom, but she hadn't found time between traveling back and forth from the States to Eastern Europe with her husband, Gary. Having adopted three kids from Yugoslavia, Ann and Gary had their hands full—and then there was the successful non-profit foundation they'd started.

Though the Fifties Chix' monthly phone call was coming up in only three days, Maxine couldn't wait and she picked up the phone and dialed her friend.

Bev whistled. "Take a break!"

The softball players high-fived each other and stretched. This was shaping up to be their best season ever, with an award-winning coach and team. It was likely they'd make it to the college championships for the third year in a row.

"Hey, Cuz," she greeted Maxine. They'd taken to calling each other that.

"You heard the news?"

"Yeah, Judy getting married. Who would have thunk it?" Bev laughed. "I guess that means she's finally over Bob."

"How is he doing?" Maxine lowered her voice. It was a tone she used a lot in Washington when colleagues were embroiled in scandal, divorce, or both.

"He'll be fine. He knew what he was getting into when he married Diane. I'm just sorry the kids have to go through their messy divorce. I'm sure they'll be spending lots of time with Aunt Bev. Anyway, enough about Bob. How are you? How's Cooper and how's the bill?"

"Coop is wonderful; his restaurant got rave reviews in *The Washington Post* and he's keeping me well-fed! As for the bill, we're getting lots of support from the House; it's the Senate I'm worried about."

"Well if anyone knows how to bend Washington to her will to do the right thing, it's you," Bev laughed. Then she covered the phone. "Clark! You and the rest of the team: ten laps, then head for the showers!"

"Conrad isn't around, is he?" Maxine asked. Bev could hear her shuffling papers, multitasking. It was like talking to Mary on the phone. Or Ann, or Judy.

"No, he's at work in the History Department. Looking forward to his sabbatical to write his Civil War book with Auntie Em." As they talked, Bev did a little multitasking herself and walked the bases, picking up stray softballs and putting them in a big neon green net bag. "I'm thinking of taking time off to go with them back to St. Louis."

"Good for you!" Maxine encouraged. Bev heard her other line buzz. "Bev, I gotta take this. It's the Senator. But say hi to Conrad for me and we'll all talk in a few days, right?"

"Right, and see you in less than a month after that. Go get 'em!"

Sometimes Mary wished the gold watch could actually tell time; she never wanted to be a minute late to the Fifties Chix conference calls. Even if Judy was always last to call in, Mary didn't want to miss a thing. She always had a plan for the grandkids and students to be occupied so she could enjoy the call undisturbed. If James wasn't traveling for work, he made sure she had her peace and quiet.

When she'd get off the call, he'd grab them both a tall glass of lemonade like the old days and wait to hear all the latest news. He never did remember the events of Mary's first "journey" to the future, but he'd been privy to many others throughout the years and had even woken up with his wife in other eras on several occasions.

Mary listened to the hold music on the special conference line they'd obtained just for these purposes. Her other line clicked and she looked at the caller ID. Her younger sister Maggie. Would she never learn that this was Mary's conference call time? Everyone who knew Mary knew she was unquestionably unavailable at this time every month. Both of Mary's sisters had plenty of mini-dramas to keep them busy between their four kids each; and with Mary's and James's two kids plus grandkids, there was never a dull moment.

At last Maggie's call in stopped dinging and Ann came on to the conference call. They exchanged warm greetings, trying to save any big news for when the others came on the call. But Ann slipped and mentioned Judy's "big news."

"The wedding? I know, I can't believe it," Mary said, brushing her white hair out of her green eyes. She took a sip of tea. Today, she had no activities to finish up while she chatted; she was just 100% "present" with her friends.

"No, there's more!" Ann said just as Judy clicked on.

"More what?" Judy asked, breathlessly. Last time she'd called in, she'd been running through Heathrow Airport, late for a flight.

At last, Bev and Maxine joined them and Judy could tell her big news. "My documentary has been nominated for an award at Cannes; there's even Oscar talk!"

Her friends squealed with delight. There were many phone calls that they could all remember: Maxine passing the bar, Mary's first baby, Bev helping write and pass Title IX, Ann's charity for Slavic orphans getting international recognition. Then there were the sad times: when Judy's step-brother and Mary's brother Danny had been killed in Vietnam; when Ann and Gary had lost their home to a devastating tornado; when Maxine's husband Cooper had been unjustly held for questioning to scare Maxine off from defending a young girl in a civil suit against the state (and, no, Maxine had not been scared off); when James had been on a writing assignment embedded with troops in Afghanistan and had gone missing. He had ultimately been fine, but it had been the longest two weeks of Mary's life and Maxine and Ann had come to stay with her. Or when Bob and Judy had finally broken up for good and her friends ached for her crushed heart.

"Do you realize what day it is?" Judy said suddenly.

"Of course," Maxine said.

"Absolutely," Ann hooted.

"Oh my goodness!" Mary yelled. "And I'm the one with the watch! May 5, 2010. We made it!"

"We're all meeting up in St. Louis for her retirement party at the end of this month," Bev insisted. "Right?"

"Right!" They agreed.

"I can't believe it's finally time to tell Mrs. F the details of our first time travel adventure and about the life she never had. Everyone have their parts down?" Mary said.

As usual, they laughed gently at her constant need to organize and orchestrate. How could they possibly forget to have written down and memorized their memoirs for Mrs. F's retirement party when Mary had emailed them about it every other day? One of the things they loved about Mary was her predictability; a welcome offshoot of which was her reliability as a friend.

"And my fiancé wants to take a look at our stories and look into buying the rights. I might finally get this film about the Fifties Chix made," Judy piped up. The other four made cheering sounds and followed up with lots of questions about Judy's fiancé. An award-winning film producer ten years her junior who was just as passionate as Judy about telling the true stories of people around the world who didn't have advocates, Robert
—

"His name is *Robert*?" Bev hooted.

"I know; can you believe it?" Judy groaned.

—Robert had fallen in love with Judy at first sight years earlier at a fundraising event for Ann and Gary's orphanage and had been pursuing her ever since.

"And I do love him," Judy said and they all heard her as a lovestruck fifteen-year-old all over again.

"I can't wait to see you all in person," said Mary, her eyes filling with tears.

Maxine said, "Friends forever, right?"

And they all agreed: "Till the end of time."

"This is all your fault, you know," said Tommy Twigler, shielding his eyes from the blazing sun and staring up into the sky.

"It most certainly is not. You're the one who gifted her the lessons!" May reminded him with a grin. As if either of them could have stopped Row once she had made up her mind to fly. "Wally, honey, climb down off that fence and come over here. Your mama's about to fly over."

Little toe-headed Wally, named for his mama's brother and dad, toddled over and slipped his hand in his Aunt May's and her heart skipped a beat. For the little rascal that he was, he could turn her to mush with those pudgy hands and that sparkling smile. She put her hand on her belly. Just two more months and Wally would have a playmate.

She caught a glimpse of her bare wrist and thought of the words that were engraved on the watch she'd used to wear there: *Liebe kann nicht nach der Zeit enthalten sein. Die Liebe ist ewig.* That is, *Love can not be contained by time. Love is forever.*

She didn't need the watch to remind her of that fact, and her life was more magical than any adventure she had ever summoned with the watch. Still, she wondered how Mary was faring with it. She'd had it for five years now and Mary and the others were enjoying their first year of college. May hoped that someday Mary would tell her about some of their time travel adventures; not because she missed the watch, but because she cared about her former students and felt a motherly bond with them.

Twig must have sensed the happiness radiating from his wife's best friend. "I'm glad you had the good sense to make up with Reggie."

"Now, don't start, Twig."

"I mean it! He adores you. You're meant to have a long, happy life together. With lots of kids." Twig suddenly looked uncomfortable and rearranged the hat on his head. His forte was jokes, not tender moments. Although since proposing to and marrying Row and having Wally, he'd gotten better at those, too.

"You first," quipped May. She knew Twig and Row looked forward to filling Row's family's old house with ankle biters.

"Working on it," Twig grinned, ruffling his son's silken hair.

"Yoohoo! Did I miss it?" Em came dashing from the parking lot toward the runway where Twig, May, and even Wally stared patiently upward.

"No, no, she's coming soon, though," May said.

"I'm so proud of our Row. An aviatrix! As soon as that baby comes, May, you know you and I have to go up with her!" Em had come straight from her dance school and had forgotten to put on shoes; now she was barefoot, her ballet slippers in one hand as she held her hat in place with the other. She looped her arm through May's elbow like she'd used to do when they were so much younger.

"That's true friendship: going up in a plane with a person when she's barely gotten her license," remarked Twig admirably.

"Oh, it's true friendship, all right," laughed Em, poking May.

"Look! There she is!"

The little white plane looked like it teetered a little as it approached; May imagined Row looking down to see and wave to her loved ones when she should have been steering. She laughed. The plane rumbled by, filling May from the top of her head down to her toes with a deep satisfying grumble, then streaked back up toward the sun. The noise, the painfully beautiful blue of the sky, the baby on its way, and her friends together and happy; the combination of all the loveliness brought tears to May's eyes. She had to shield her eyes from the brightness of the sun, yet she couldn't bear to look away from the dazzling scene: it was the glorious image of all their dreams coming true.

She felt a kick in her belly and her heart caught. Sometimes Marion Fairview wondered how different life would have been if they had never found Emily. Glancing at Em, who was laughing and pointing into the sky, standing elegantly in her tippy toes like the ballerina she was, May dismissed the notion. She and Row *had* found Emily; and whatever life threw at them, they'd face it together as forever friends.

22

Die Liebe ist ewig

Mary

Mary took good care of Nana and her sisters, brother, and mom. She wanted her home to be a place where her friends could come and find peace and comfort and laughter. So when James confided in her that his parents were splitting up, she made sure he knew he'd always have a place with her family when he was feeling down. The following school year, he'd even gotten to live with his Aunt Row and eventually Aunt Row had a family of her own, in which she was sure to include James.

Mary's dad married Tiffani and they had three children of their own. Mary spent much of the rest of high school babysitting them—that is, when she wasn't having adventures with her friends, studying hard, or proofreading James's writing and encouraging him. James proposed when Mary was a senior in college and James was working at the local paper. They got married three months after Nana and her beau of six months tied the knot.

Mary and James took their time starting a family, as they had plenty of adventures together with Mary's watch and felt no rush to settle down. They dreamed of someday writing the great American novel together about their "travels." Then the day came when Mary announced that she was expecting and baby Jimmy arrived in the spring. Only a couple of years later, his little sister Jane arrived.

Both Mary and James loved teaching their little ones and did so at every opportunity that they could find. While James's writing career expanded, taking him overseas, Mary began a school in their home for Jimmy's and Jane's friends and cousins.

Mary's life was rich and happy—more so than she'd ever thought it could be; and at the top of her list of blessings were four names: Judy, Maxine, Beverly, and Ann.

"Travel to Tomorrow"
Mary Jane Donovan
Fifth Period - Miss Boggs
Social Studies
May 4, 1955

History repeats itself, but eventually mankind learns from its mistakes. Each generation improves from the last. Technology, innovation and education create strides forward. While in 1955 we live in a complicated post-war era with shifting social values, fifty years from now, we will enjoy the fruits of technology, innovation, and education in a finer way. Concepts that are now abstractions will become reality. Home life will reflect the advancement of the age.

In the new millennium, families will enjoy the benefits of technology, making home life easier. Housewives will find more time to put into their children and husband's well being by the liberation from housecleaning, done by magnetic forces and robots. Cooking will be a snap with instant baking techniques, and many meals will come in the form of a pill. Robots will control the temperature of households and turn the lights on and off at a command.

Because of robots and futuristic technology, businessmen will have shortened work days to spend more time with family. This will result in a stronger family unit and fewer incidents of divorce, as well as improved family finances.

Overall, the future is bright for families and children. Because of social and technological improvements, the future will be a simpler time.

Judy

When Judy got the lead role as Lizzie that summer, her friends cheered her on in the front row just as they had promised—right along with Roger Streeter, who proposed to Judy's mom the next day. By Christmas, Judy had two little stepbrothers. And she had gone steady with Bob twice and broken it off twice.

It wasn't until after she graduated from acting school in Los Angeles in 1962 that she realized she'd have to leave the real-life drama of Bob Jenkins in order to devote her life to drama on stage and on film. She had been fine until Bob, who had never been ready to fully commit to Judy, married Diane Dunkelman less than a year later. Heartbroken, she vowed to her friends she would never love again.

It appeared she wouldn't have had time to love, because her career took off. Finding it harder and harder to find significant roles, Judy began to champion projects that had deeper social messages, inspired in part by all that her friends were doing. Time and again, she came up against resistance when she pitched movie ideas to her agent and rep, even when she had the money to supplement production cost. It appeared that unless she married someone powerful, she wouldn't find a way to get her movies made.

Instead, she partnered with influential writers and directors and started her own production house. Even then, it was decades before Judy finally made a movie in which she was proud to feature her name under the producing byline. It was a sci-fi epic featuring a group of boys who time traveled. Judy promised the universe that someday, whether the world was ready or not, she'd tell the real story: that it had been five girls who'd time traveled.

May 4, 1955
Travel To Tomorrow-Entertainment and Popular Culture
Judy E. White
Social Studies
Miss Boggs

In the new century, we will see film and television going beyond entertainment and being a force for education, Hollywood stars will be pillars in the international community, leaders, because they share their artistic talent to help improve the world.

Since the beginning of time, cultures have progressed and strengthened their traditions through story telling. In the future, the importance of story telling will be just as important, but the medium will have evolved. Movies and television will be the main avenues of story telling, maintaining social values and messages while simultaneously entertaining the masses. As Shakespeare's plays educated and entertained even the commoners, movies and television shows will have a broad impact in shaping and defining the culture of the future.

Due to the increasing significance of the entertainment industry and its role in society, actors and writers will be at a premium and highly regarded as artists and leaders.

Maxine

When Melba came home from college for summer break, Maxine became her shadow, asking incessant questions about what Mel and her classmates were doing about the civil rights issue and how Maxine could become involved. When Mel went to visit her ex-boyfriend, Cooper Brown, in prison, Maxine asked to come along. Her parents flatly refused, but after a solid three months of pleading, she wore them down. Maxine accompanied Mel on Mel's last visit to Cooper before she headed back to school.

Over the years, as Mel lost interest in Coop, Maxine's visits increased. She marveled at Coop's resilience and faith in humanity, despite being unjustly locked up for robbing a store a gunpoint—a store Coop had never set foot in. They promised each other they'd attend marches and rallies in the south when he got out. Maxine knew she wanted to meet Dr. Martin Luther King, Jr. before he was unfairly and tragically taken from the world in April 1968.

When Maxine started looking at colleges to attend, she brought the literature to show Coop to encourage him to continue his education, too. He was the first one to suggest she look into pre-law, insisting that he and others like him needed a good lawyer.

In the middle of her sophomore year in college, Coop showed up on campus to surprise her: he'd been paroled two years early. When he asked her dad's permission for her hand in marriage, a fight ensued between Maxine and her family that made Mel's old quarrels with their mama seem like a walk in the park. Her parents would not have her "marry a convict." Now Maxine understood firsthand the resistance Bev and Conrad were up against as a couple in a prejudiced society and admired that the more resistance they faced, the deeper they dug in.

The result was that Maxine Marshall-Brown would be one of the first lawyers to have a case retried and have her client, Cooper Marshall-Brown, exonerated with DNA testing.

And through it all, even when her family took a step back from her when the outcome looked grim, her friends never did.

Travel To Tomorrow—World Events/Politics
Maxine Marshall
Social Studies
Miss Boggs
5-4-55

The future is bound to be a simpler time.
Since the birth of these great United States,
men and women of all colors have struggled
for equality. Negroes and women had to work
for the same rights as white men. Progress
has been slow but sure. In 50 years, we will
see even more progress.

The world will be color-blind and we'll see
the law and human rights as universal, not
just applying to one particular race. For example, since it will be more than fifty years
since the Brown versus Board of Education
Supreme Court decision about integrating
schools, everyone will have the same
opportunities for education, no matter what
shade their skin is. No one has to go to a
different school because of the color of

*their skin or even because they're girls. Every-
one will have a vote and everyone will have
equal pay.*

*World events will focus not so much on
war-like acts, but on common projects and a
broad, thriving world economy. Peoples of the
world will not be divided by their differences,
but united by their talents and generosity.*

Bev

Bev could appreciate her friends' newfound optimism when they arrived back in 1955—and if not sheer optimism, as in Maxine's case, a glimmer of hope—but Bev resented the one thing she was forced to master: patience. While Mary and Ann may have had to take things slow in approaching James and Gary, Bev—for her own and Conrad's safety—had to move at a glacial pace—that is, at society's pace.

When Conrad's Aunt Em moved back to town, she advocated for Conrad and Bev; and when she married Bev's Uncle Petey, Bev and Conrad each had a legitimate excuse to meet at their house for dinner. Bev even became a fan of babysitting since it was another reason to "run into" Conrad there. Seeing Uncle Petey and Em graciously navigate reactions to their relationship fortified Bev's resolve—although most folks didn't realize Em was part African American, so it wasn't quite the same.

Still, Bev longed for the day when she and Conrad could go to a ballgame or play pinball at a diner, or appear anywhere in public as a couple. When Bev's parents caught on to her attachment to Conrad, they were scandalized. They insisted they were concerned for her and how "society" would make life difficult for her. It would take years before they truly attempted to get to know Conrad and by then, Bev wondered if it was too late to salvage her relationship with them.

At every turn, Bev's fondest hopes and dreams were met with hostility, whether it was playing athletics or dating Conrad Marshall . . . or, later, marrying him. Of course, not *every* turn: there was Aunt Em, her brother Gary with his newfound religious pacifism, and her four best friends. She had to credit them with giving her the inspiration that kept her going in her work to help draft Title IX and pass it when it became a bill. And ironically, none of them even played sports.

But more than anyone she knew, the Fifties Chix knew how to be a team.

May 4, 1955
Beverly Jenkins
Travel To Tomorrow-Athletics
Social Studies with Miss Boggs

Year after year, mankind and womankind have been excelling and progressing in athletics. Records are broken every year as people put off physical limits. Women will excel in professional leagues just as men do and girls will have opportunities in school to exercise their athletic abilities.

Society will come to discover that it is no less lady-like for a female to excel in athletics than it is for her to excel in other areas of life like home economy. Exercise will continue to be an important part of a healthy life, and perhaps even more important with the advances in technology that means robots may do much more of the manual labor that mankind--and woman kind--is used to doing.

Athletics will continue to be a form of entertainment, but will be more inclusive of women athletes. The All-American Girls Professional Baseball League will be restarted with better funding and broader fan support and many fine women athletes from which to choose.

By incorporating more athletics into girls' education, more professional level women players will be available. Then things like the All-American Girls Professional Baseball League will not be a footnote in history, but the model for many other women's sports leagues and women will have more choices than just being a mother if that's not what they want to do.

Ann

Ann had thought the first sock hop with Gary back in 1955 had been a tickle, but she was stunned when he asked if he could come to temple with her the following Saturday before the next sock hop. Gary loved it, and even when he and Ann were going steady later on, she warned him she wouldn't continue to date him just because he wanted to convert. He said he wanted to practice Judaism with or without her, but if wearing a yarmulke meant he'd more likely be with her, it was that much more appealing.

While Ann's parents were thrilled, Gary's weren't. Bev's friendship with a black boy had them beside themselves with worry, and in addition to that, their business was struggling. In 1960, the Jenkins let Ann's mom go from being their house-keeper. While part of it could have legitimately been because their financial situation had changed when they brought in Bev's uncle Pete as part owner of Jenkins Hardware, Ann couldn't help but think that it may have been due to a bit of resentment that Gary had so readily taken to Ann's family and their culture and religion.

Just as Gary had said once upon a time that he would, he did go to Belgrade, accompanied by Ann. She had told him about her grandmother's painting and she wanted to find it, as well as meet Irina in person. It proved to be their first of many trips to the Balkans together to find art; and they rushed to get married before either of them was finished with college because they had fallen in love with two orphaned toddlers and wanted to bring them home to start a family. Their family continued to expand into a charity placing other orphans with American families, including Bev's and Conrad's.

Every time Ann kissed the top of some precious child's head and wished him or her well in a new family, or her heart hurt trying to find him or her a home, she wondered how she could ever be living a life so sweet and rich if it hadn't been for her glimpse into another dimension with her best friends. Life continued to surprise her, but her friends' loyalty and encouragement remained constant.

4 May, 1955

Ann Branislav

Travel To Tomorrow-Art in the Future

Social Studies - Miss Boggs

Every day the sun rises and sets, giving its lovely glow to the earth. And every day an artist is inspired to record her impressions of beautiful nature in the poetry of paint and color. The future holds the promise of uncensored expression through art, writing and drama. Books won't be burned or banned any more and art will be a regular part of education and a big part of everyone's lives. Artists and educators of the future will be honored and highly regarded.

My wish is for everyone to have the eye of the artist—to see beauty in surprising places, to find love where you least expect it, and to live life as the divine masterpiece that it truly is. ∽

Glossary

110 in the Shade: A musical that came out in 1967 (and was revived thirty years later) based on the 1954 play *The Rainmaker* by N. Richard Nash. About a "spinster" named Lizzie Curry who falls under the spell of a charismatic conman named Starbuck.

Ankle biters: kids

Beat: cool, a Beatnik quality

Beatnik: A young person associated with the subculture called the "beat generation," a movement inspired by Jack Kerouac. "Beat" comes from the word "Beatitude." Beatniks were known for wearing black turtlenecks, sunglasses, and berets.

Big tickle: so funny!

Cloud nine: heaven

Fream: a freak or a misfit

Hepcat: a cool dude or a cool chick

In orbit: in the know, in the loop

Goof: a clown or a fool; someone who messes up a lot

Grody: gross, not cool

Mary's Meatloaf Recipe (makes 6 servings)

❈ 3/4 cup hot milk
❈ 2 cups soft bread crumbs
❈ 2 pounds ground beef
❈ 1 cup chopped onion
❈ 2 teaspoons salt
❈ 1 teaspoon poultry seasoning
❈ 1/2 teaspoon pepper
❈ 1/4 teaspoon ground cloves
❈ 3 eggs, beaten

Pour hot milk over crumbs. Combine remaining ingredients. Stir into milk mixture. Bake in greased 9-1/2×5-1/4x-2-3/4 inch loaf pan at 350° (moderate) for 1 hour. (from Recipe-Curio.com)

Phosphate: a "soft drink" made of phosphoric acid and often flavored with fruit; the soda pops we drink these days in bottles and cans are essentially phosphates

Red-light-green-light: When a car full of people stops at a red light, everyone gets out and runs around the car to a new spot before the light turns green. Anyone not back in the car gets left behind!

Soda jerk: a kid who works at a drugstore or five-and-dime mixing soda fountain drinks (shakes, sodas, and phosphates, for example) and serving ice cream

BE KEPT IN ORBIT, HEP CATS!

Look for these other titles in the Fifties Chix series:

Book 1: Travel to Tomorrow

Book 2: Keeping Secrets

Book 3: Third Time's a Charm

Book 4: Broken Record

Go to http://FiftiesChix.com and join the Fan Club for updates on the Fifties Chix book series, more info on your fave characters, secret diary entries, contests, and more!

Also check out the Fifties Chix Book Club and Lit Guide at **http://fiftieschix.com/lit-guide** for extended activities and fun writing resources!

BOOK 1

travel to tomorrow

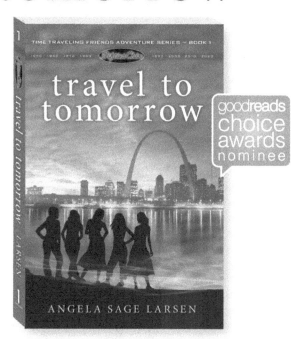

Sock hops. Soda fountains. Slumber parties. Life in 1955 is simple for tomboy Beverly, moody Maxine, high-spirited Judy, studious Mary and artistic Ann. But after a class assignment to predict life in the future, they wake up the next morning in a future they could never have imagined (having time-traveled into a parallel universe to the 21st century. With only each other to trust, they must work together and find their way "home" to 1955; but the more they discover about the future, will they even want to go back?

SIGN UP TO GET UPDATES, PARTICIPATE IN FAN CLUB ACTIVITIES & GET SNEAK PREVIEWS OF UPCOMING EVENTS AT FIFTIESCHIX.COM

Book 2

keeping
secrets

THE MYSTERY UNFOLDS IN A FUTURE LINKED TO THE PAST
THROUGH SECRETS THAT MUST NOW BE UNCOVERED AND TOLD.

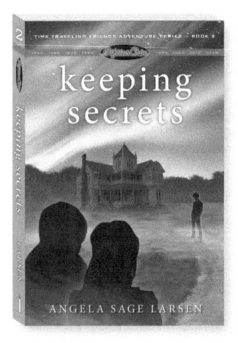

As if their quest to return home isn't challenging enough for Fifties Chix friends Mary, Ann, Judy, Maxine, and Bev – they must also cope with a love triangle between Mary, Ann and James O'Grady; the unexplained disappearance of their classroom teacher; and the revealing essay Maxine writes for the school's underground newspaper.

Hang on tight as the time-traveling quintet explodes through well-kept secrets to find the answers in the second book of the Fifties Chix series.

SIGN UP TO GET UPDATES, PARTICIPATE IN FAN CLUB ACTIVITIES & GET SNEAK PREVIEWS OF UPCOMING EVENTS AT FIFTIESCHIX.COM

BOOK 3

1950　1960　1970　1980　1990　2000　2010　2020

third time's a charm

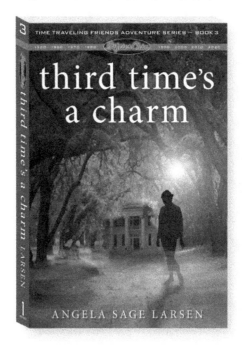

In 1945 May Boggs, the Fifties Chix' social studies teacher, is 15 years old. World War II has taken its toll and May and her two best friends, Rowena and Emily, are happy to see the war coming to an end at long last. But their bright futures are disrupted by a trip back to another war torn era – the Civil War.

When in modern day, Maxine pays the price for the controversial essay she wrote for the school's underground paper, the secret her teacher uncovers in 1864 may be the very thing that saves Maxine's – and the Fifties Chix' – reputation and future.

SIGN UP TO GET UPDATES, PARTICIPATE IN FAN CLUB ACTIVITIES & GET SNEAK PREVIEWS OF UPCOMING EVENTS AT FIFTIESCHIX.COM

Book 4

broken record

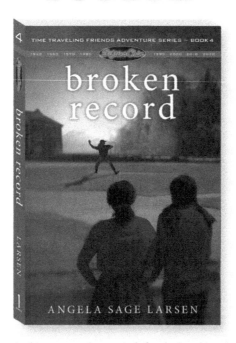

When Bev is recruited in present day to pitch for the boys' baseball team, she is in seventh heaven when her team could earn its way to the championship game. Standing between Bev and victory is her arch nemesis, Diane Dunkelman. She must come to terms once and for all with her rival, and learn how to follow her heart about the boy she likes. In sports as in life, Bev discovers, she must be true to herself to win. Meanwhile, Ann, Mary, Maxine and Judy are on the trail of a mysterious, reclusive friend from their social studies teacher's past who may have the secret to their time-traveling dilemma. Get ready to cheer for the Fifties Chix as their time-travel journey leads them on unexpected twists and turns toward victory in the fourth book of the series.

SIGN UP TO GET UPDATES, PARTICIPATE IN FAN CLUB ACTIVITIES & GET SNEAK PREVIEWS OF UPCOMING EVENTS AT FIFTIESCHIX.COM

Premiere

http://premiere.fastpencil.com